Zero Hour

MARK WALDEN

BLOOMSBURY

LONDON · BERLIN · NEW YORK · SYDNEY

Bloomsbury Publishing, London, Berlin, New York and Sydney

First published in Great Britain in September 2010 by Bloomsbury Publishing Plc
36 Soho Square, London, W1D 3QY

This paperback edition first published in August 2011

A CIP catalogue record of this book is available from the British Library

ISBN 978 1 4088 1595 3

FSC
www.fsc.org
MIX
Paper from
responsible sources
FSC® C018072

Typeset by Dorchester Typesetting Group Ltd
Printed in Great Britain by Clays Ltd, St Ives Plc, Bungay, Suffolk

1 3 5 7 9 10 8 6 4 2

www.bloomsbury.com
www.hivehub.co.uk

For Greybeard the Stupid Pirate

chapter one

A thin, elderly-looking man sat in a darkened office, facing an array of screens. At first glance a casual observer might have thought that he was ill, but closer inspection would have revealed the fine black veins covering his skin. Nothing was left of the man who had once inhabited this shell – all that mattered now was that it belonged to Overlord.

Overlord watched as the screens lit up one by one with the digitally distorted faces of his most loyal followers: men and women who had honoured his legacy and continued the work he had begun while imprisoned inside the body of another. His Disciples.

'Good evening, ladies and gentlemen,' he said. 'I have called this meeting to discuss a very important matter. I have reviewed the plans that you initiated during my enforced absence and, while many are impractical, one has true potential. Its code name is Tabula Rasa and although its scope is currently rather limited I believe that with some simple modifications it can be made . . . *effective*.'

'Master,' one of the faces said, 'what can we do to assist?'

'The facility which contains the substance we require is quite secure,' Overlord replied. 'I believe that Furan can provide the manpower necessary to handle that side of the plan but we will also need to address the greatest threat to our success, G.L.O.V.E.'

G.L.O.V.E., the Global League of Villainous Enterprise, was an organisation that had once been entirely under his control. That was, quite literally, in a previous lifetime. Now it was under the control of Maximilian Nero, a man who had been a thorn in Overlord's side for far too long.

'We can eliminate that threat,' Overlord continued, 'but I shall need your assistance. I am sending you details of a number of key G.L.O.V.E. facilities around the world. When I give the signal you are to attack and destroy them. I, meanwhile, will put into action a plan to eliminate G.L.O.V.E.'s leaders in one fell swoop. I will transmit the details of your targets to all of you shortly so that you may make your preparations. Our time is coming, ladies and gentlemen. Soon we shall remake the Earth in our image and there will be no one to stand against us.'

The screens went blank again and Pietor Furan stepped forward out of the shadows.

'I do not mean to question you,' Furan said, 'but Tabula Rasa was one of our more extreme initiatives. I take it that you have an idea for how we can modulate its destructive power?'

'Of course I do,' Overlord replied, 'but to do it we need one last piece of the puzzle. We need Otto Malpense and I know exactly how we're going to get him.'

☣ ☣ ☣

Otto ducked behind the low wall, trying to control his breathing, his ears straining for any sign of his pursuers. He knew that they were out there but all he could hear was the slow drip of water from a leaking pipe nearby. Raising himself up just far enough to look over the wall, he scanned the wide open concrete floor of the abandoned warehouse. The only illumination was provided by the dirty cracked skylights far overhead. He crept out, moving as quickly and quietly as possible from one area of shadow to the next. Suddenly he heard the crunch of someone stepping on loose gravel and he flattened himself against the wall, raising his silenced pistol to shoulder level, ready to fire.

A shadowy figure rounded the corner and just had time to grunt with surprise as Otto's pistol coughed twice, the shots catching his target square in the chest. The hunter slumped to the floor with a thud and Otto broke into a run. He knew that in the silence of the deserted building even the suppressed sound of his shots would have given away his position. He was halfway towards the other side of the open area when a bullet buzzed past his head and hit the wall twenty metres away with a puff of ancient plaster dust. He dived and rolled behind a wooden crate, knowing full well that the shelter it provided was temporary at best. As if to hammer that message home another bullet passed through the crate in an explosion of splinters just centimetres from his head and struck the ground nearby. He looked desperately for anything that would provide him with more substantial cover and spotted a concrete support column about ten metres away. To reach it he would have to cross open ground.

Time seemed to slow down as he glanced at the splintered hole in the crate and the tiny crater in the concrete floor where the bullet had ricocheted away. He subconsciously calculated the trajectory of the bullet, his mind drawing a line back from the crater and through the crate. Springing up from behind the crate, he sighted his pistol and fired three times. There was a scream of pain from somewhere off in the darkness and Otto sprinted for the comparative safety of the column. He pressed his back against the pillar, listening for signs of pursuit but hearing nothing. Suddenly there was a flicker of movement from off to his right and he spun round, raising his weapon. He gasped as he felt a sudden sharp pain in his chest and looking down he saw the silver hilt of a throwing knife protruding from the centre of his chest. He collapsed to his knees, his pistol falling from his numb fingers, and as the darkness swallowed him he saw a familiar figure detach itself from the shadows nearby and walk towards him.

'I am sorry, my friend,' Wing said, looking down at him as Otto lost consciousness.

There was a sudden flash of white light and the warehouse seemed to melt away to be replaced by a brightly lit cave with a smooth metal floor.

'Exercise terminated,' H.I.V.E.mind said calmly. 'Holographic projectors and variable geometry forcefields offline.'

Otto rose groggily to his feet, feeling his strength gradually returning.

'There is such a thing as too realistic, you know,' he said, rubbing at his sternum and trying to forget the pain and shock that he had felt just a few moments before.

'That's the whole point, Mr Malpense,' Colonel Francisco said, striding across the empty cavern as Wing helped Otto to his feet. 'The neural feedback suit allows you to feel all of the pain without suffering any of the physical injury. It ensures you take these training sessions seriously.'

That may have been the proper name for the bodysuit that Otto was wearing but he definitely preferred the nickname that it had earned among the students of H.I.V.E. – the Agoniser.

'Good work, Mr Fanchu,' Francisco said. 'You took your target down without hesitation but I would still rather see you using your side arms.'

'It was not necessary,' Wing replied with a slight shake of the head.

'Well, one day it might be,' Francisco replied with a frown. 'Let's hope you won't hesitate then. The end result is the same, after all.'

Wing gave a small nod. Otto understood very well why his friend had not used his gun. The first and only time that Wing had shot somebody it had been his own father. He had saved Otto's life but had still not forgiven himself for killing Cypher and breaking the solemn vow he had once made to his mother never to take a life.

'Thanks a lot, Otto,' Shelby said as she walked towards them, rubbing her shoulder. 'When the hell did you become such a good shot?'

'Beginner's luck,' Otto replied with a shrug.

'And did you really have to shoot me twice?' Laura asked, still looking slightly groggy from being rendered temporarily unconscious by the neural shock administered by her own Agoniser suit.

'You gave away your position, Miss Brand,' Francisco said with a slight shake of his head. 'How many times do I have to tell you about watching where you're walking?'

'Sorry, Colonel,' Laura sighed. 'I'll do better next time.'

'Let's hope you do,' Francisco replied. 'Out in the real world there won't be a next time. H.I.V.E.mind, please upload the result of today's exercise to the central academic server.'

'Upload complete,' H.I.V.E.mind replied.

'Good. That's all for now, ladies and gentlemen,' the Colonel said. 'We'll be moving on to wilderness environments next week, so please review the tactical briefings on your terminals. Dismissed.'

Otto, Wing, Laura and Shelby met in the assembly area five minutes later after changing out of the neural feedback suits and into their black Alpha stream jumpsuits. They were just about to head back to their accommodation block when the doors on the other side of the room hissed open and Lucy, Franz and Nigel walked towards them.

'How did it go?' Laura asked Lucy, noting the slight scowl on the other girl's face.

'Don't ask,' Lucy said with a sigh.

'I am thinking that you will be wanting to tell the

others of my glorious victory,' Franz said with a huge, beaming smile.

'OK, OK.' Lucy winced.

'Franz won?' Shelby asked, trying hard to not sound too astonished.

'Yes,' Franz replied proudly. 'I am being like the shadow in the night. They can run but they cannot hide.'

'You got lucky,' Nigel said, sounding slightly irritated.

'Luck is not being the factor,' Franz said, shaking his head. 'I am just being too good for you.'

'Well,' Otto said with a grin, 'I for one want to hear all about it.'

'It does indeed sound like a glorious victory,' Wing said. Even he was struggling to keep a straight face.

'I'm not going to be allowed to forget about this in a hurry, am I?' Lucy said as Franz walked out of the room with Otto and Wing, explaining in great detail how his extraordinary stealth and cunning had been instrumental in defeating his opponents.

'Don't worry – there's no shame in losing,' Shelby replied.

'Really?' Lucy asked hopefully.

Shelby burst out laughing, setting Laura off too.

'I think this is going to be a very long day,' Nigel said to Lucy with a sigh.

☻ ☻ ☻

Three men sat in a crowded bar in Colorado, a frosted half-full pitcher of beer on the table between them. The first man raised his glass.

'A toast, guys, to the MWP-X1 and the brave, intelligent and handsome men that are gonna show the world what it can do tomorrow.'

'I'll drink to that,' the second man said, raising his glass.

'It's going to take more than one glass of beer for me to find either one of you two freaks handsome, but ah, what the hell!' the third man said, raising his glass.

'Let's just hope that the General doesn't find out that we're not all tucked up in our bunks,' the second man said with a grin. 'I'm not sure that this is what he meant by a good night's rest.'

'Well, he can't throw us in the brig till after the demonstration,' the first man said, 'so I guess we'll be OK for the next twenty-four hours.'

'After twelve months of living in the desert with him barking orders at us every day, I figure that's the least he owes us,' the third man replied.

'You better not be complaining, son,' the first man said, putting on a gruff Southern accent, 'because you should be proud – proud to be a part of the future of this great nation's armed forces.'

'Sir, yes sir,' the second man said, saluting the other man with a grin.

The three of them sat chatting and laughing for another half an hour. None of the other people in the bar would have guessed by looking at them that they were the test pilots for one of the most confidential advanced military research projects on the planet.

'We should get going,' the third man said eventually, finishing his beer. 'It's gonna be an early start in the morning.'

'It's an early start every morning,' the first man said with a sigh as he too finished his drink, 'but yeah, I guess you're right.'

'We better get some R & R after the demo tomorrow,' the second man said. 'I've had enough desert to last me a lifetime.'

The three men got up from the table and left the bar, walking out into the cool night air and crossing the parking lot.

'What the hell –' the first man said angrily as they rounded the corner of the building. A shadowy figure was standing beside his truck, working a long thin bar down between the rubber seal and the glass of the driver's side window. 'Hey! Get away from my truck!' he yelled.

The thief's head snapped round and he saw the three men sprinting towards him. Abandoning his attempt to break into the vehicle, he ran into the darkness beyond the edge of the lot with the others in close pursuit. They gained on him quickly as they sprinted across the dusty scrubland and when the first of them got to within a couple of metres he dived forward, hitting his target in the small of the back with his shoulder and bringing him to the ground with a crunching thud. He rolled the thief on to his back and put one knee on the struggling man's chest.

'You picked the wrong truck to steal, buddy,' the first man said as his two companions pinned the thief's arms to the ground.

'Actually,' the other man said with a smile, 'it was precisely the right truck.'

There were three small coughing sounds from somewhere behind the men and each of them felt a sudden sharp sting on the back of their neck. The thief caught the first man by the shoulders as he fell forward unconscious, and his two companions collapsed to the desert floor beside him. The thief stood up, brushing the dust from his jeans as three figures wearing black combat fatigues and night-vision goggles appeared from the darkness, lowering their tranquilliser dart guns and walking towards the unconscious men on the ground.

'Good work,' Pietor Furan said as he pushed the goggles up on to the top of his head. The smiling thief gave a small nod.

'Get them on to the truck,' Furan said to the two men beside him. 'We don't have much time.'

�☻☻

'Ahhh, Lieutenant Barton, I'm glad to see that you're awake,' a voice said from somewhere in the darkness that surrounded him.

Barton tried to sit up but was stopped by the straps that bound him firmly to the bed.

'Who are you?' Barton asked, an edge of panic to his voice. 'How do you know my name?'

'Perfectly reasonable questions under the circumstances,' the voice replied, 'but I'm afraid that we don't have time for a full explanation. Let's just say that I am someone who is eager to ensure your full cooperation.'

'You can go to hell,' Barton said angrily.

'Your two friends had a similar reaction,' the voice replied with a sinister chuckle, 'but they soon started to see things my way.'

'What do you mean?' Barton said, feeling sudden fear for the safety of his friends. 'What have you done to them?'

'Exactly what I'm going to do to you,' the voice replied.

There was a whirring sound and a metal arm with a syringe mounted on the end moved into position next to Barton's neck. With a hiss it slid forward, plunging the

12

needle into the struggling man's artery. Barton felt a burning sensation spread across his skull as the contents of the syringe were injected.

'You have just been injected with the latest generation of a substance called Animus,' the voice explained calmly. 'You should consider yourself lucky – previous generations would have killed you instantly but this will just make you more . . . cooperative.'

Barton thrashed on the bed for a few more seconds and then his struggling subsided and he lay still, his eyes staring blankly into space.

'Good. Are you ready for your new orders?' the voice asked.

'Yes, sir,' Barton replied.

'Excellent,' the voice said. 'Now here's what you're going to do . . .'

☹ ☹ ☹

The technician lifted up the metal cover and plugged his laptop into the data port next to the cockpit, watching as the screen filled with a series of diagnostic displays. Hearing footsteps at the other end of the long gantry behind him, he glanced over his shoulder. A man in a flight suit and mirrored sunglasses walked towards the cockpit, a helmet under his arm.

'Morning, Lieutenant Barton,' the technician said.

13

'She's prepped and ready for launch. Me and the other guys all wanted to wish you the best of luck with the demonstration today.'

The pilot didn't reply as he walked past the technician and climbed into the open cockpit, buckling himself into the single seat and pulling the helmet on to his head. The technician quickly disconnected the computer as the cockpit's armoured canopy whirred down into place and locked shut with a solid thud.

'Yeah, well, excuse me for breathing, Mr High-and-Mighty fly-boy,' the technician muttered under his breath as he walked back along the gantry.

☢ ☢ ☢

General Collins walked up to the lectern and looked at the banked rows of seats filled with men and women in a mixture of business suits and military uniforms. He smiled with satisfaction at the thought of what he was about to show them.

'Ladies and gentlemen, it gives me great pleasure to welcome you all to the Advanced Weapons Project proving grounds. I appreciate the fact that many of you have accepted the invitation to this demonstration without having any idea of exactly what it is that you are going to be shown today. I hope that what you are about to see will not be a disappointment. For some time now this facility has been responsible for the research and development of cutting-edge military systems – machines that will win not only the wars of today but also the wars of tomorrow. And so it is with great pride that I welcome you this morning to the first demonstration of the next generation of mobile armoured weapons platform. Since the First World War the tank has been the dominant force on the modern battlefield, but with the advent of increasingly advanced anti-armour weapons systems it has become clear that something new was required. A vehicle that would have all of the strengths of its predecessors but none of their vulnerabilities or limitations. A vehicle that would change the very nature of warfare in the twenty-first century. Ladies and gentlemen, I am extremely proud to present . . . Goliath.'

There was a low rumble from somewhere behind the stands and then three huge shapes roared over the heads of the startled audience and landed with ground-shaking thuds on the desert floor a couple of hundred metres away. Each machine stood about thirty metres high, towering armoured metal giants with multi-barrelled Gatling cannons mounted on each arm and rocket pods on each shoulder. Positioned in the centre of each of the giant mechs' chests was a black glass cockpit shrouded in heavy armour. They walked forward, taking up position facing the crowds, the fluidity of their movement strangely at odds with their size and weight. Collins noted with satisfaction the sudden buzz of excited chatter from the assembled dignitaries.

'Goliath represents unquestioned battlefield dominance. As agile in the air as they are on land, they are a force multiplier of enormous power and versatility,' Collins continued. 'But why just tell you what they can do when we can show you instead?'

He picked up a walkie-talkie from the lectern and thumbed the transmit button.

'OK, boys, let's give these people a show.'

The Goliaths turned, facing away from the waiting audience and towards the decommissioned tanks that were positioned down-range. The first of the giant machines raised its arm and the huge rotary cannon mounted on its forearm spun up and with a buzzing roar opened fire. The derelict tank was ripped to pieces by the heavy-calibre shells, shredded pieces of twisted metal flying in all directions. The rocket pods on the shoulders of the second of the three machines rotated slightly, locking on to another one of the distant armoured vehicles. Two rockets streaked from each of the pods, trailing white exhaust plumes, slamming into the doomed target and sending flaming chunks of armour plate scattering across the desert.

'As you can see, ladies and gentlemen, the Goliath is

capable of taking out ground targets with ease, but as I'm sure you all know the greatest threat to any ground vehicle on the modern battlefield comes from the air. So let's show you how they deal with just such an airborne threat.'

High above the proving grounds the Predator drone that had been circling banked towards its preassigned target, locking on to the third Goliath far below. The Hellfire missile detached from the drone's wing, its engines igniting and sending it screaming towards the stationary mech far below. A black dome mounted on the top of the targeted Goliath spun round and fired a pencil-thin beam of high-energy laser light at the incoming missile, instantly detonating it in mid-air.

'The Goliath's anti-ballistic laser system can take out anything from a missile to an incoming artillery round or tank shell. Put simply, you can't kill what you can't hit. Of course, each unit is fully outfitted with the latest in ground-to-air weaponry, but for the sake of this demon-stration let's get a little more up close and personal.' Collins turned and nodded towards the pilot of the third machine and the vectored thrust engines on its back ignited, sending the Goliath rocketing into the sky. The members of the audience quickly picked up the binoculars they had been given and watched as the giant machine streaked towards the unmanned drone with a speed and manoeuvrability belying its size. The pilot brought the Goliath within range of the frantically weaving drone, matching its wildly evasive flight path turn for turn. The crowd watched as the giant armoured machine drew level with the Predator and then simply swatted it from the sky with a single swipe of one giant armoured fist. The blazing debris of the drone tumbled towards the desert far below.

'I hope the Air Force boys weren't expecting that one back,' Collins said with a grin, drawing an appreciative laugh from the assembled dignitaries. 'As you can see, Goliath blurs the line between ground-based and airborne weapon systems. It is truly the master of both land and sky.'

From somewhere behind the spectators came the distinctive sound of helicopter rotors and they twisted in their seats, eager to see what the next part of the demonstration would bring. Moments later three black helicopters passed low over the crowd, the downdraught from their thumping rotors kicking up clouds of dust from the desert floor. They came to a hover in front of the stands and opened their side doors, three squads of well-armed troops in black body armour rapidly climbing out and descending zip lines to the ground.

'What the hell –' Collins gasped. This was definitely not part of the demonstration. He grabbed the walkie-talkie from the lectern.

'All Goliath units cleared to engage unknown hostiles!'

he barked. 'Take these suckers out!' He waited for confirmation of his orders from the pilots of the three mechs but heard only static. 'I say again, engage unidentified hostile forces.'

The three Goliaths started to move, but instead of opening fire on the unknown soldiers who were sprinting towards the spectators they simply shifted into position alongside the helicopters as they landed fifty metres away, then raised the Gatling cannons on their arms and levelled them at the startled crowd, barrels spinning, ready to fire. Collins could do nothing but watch helplessly as the men in black raced up the stairs on either end of the grandstand and trained their rifles on the frightened spectators. A couple tried to run but were quickly overpowered and pushed to their knees, hands behind their heads. As Collins stood frozen in disbelief, a single figure climbed down from the side door of one of the helicopters and made his way up the steps to join him on the platform. As he reached Collins, he pulled a pistol from the holster on his hip and pointed it at him.

'General Collins,' he said with a smile, 'my name is Pietor Furan and this demonstration is over.'

☗ ☗ ☗

Otto woke with a start, his head buzzing with pain. Staggering to his feet, he stumbled through the darkened room, heading for the bathroom at the rear of his living quarters. He slapped the switch on the wall and bright white light blinded him for a second. As his eyes adjusted to the glare he stared at his own reflection in the mirror and a fresh bolt of pain lanced across his skull. He fought against the rising tide of nausea and disorientation, studying the pale face that looked back at him from the glass. A thin red line, like a fine cut, traced across his right cheek. Otto ran his finger along the fresh wound, feeling an unusual warmth as the gash seemed to widen and separate, then gasped in horror as it flared suddenly with red light and the skin began to peel back from his cheek, revealing what looked like blood-covered glass. He recoiled from his own reflection as more bright red lines spread across his skin, the flesh falling away to reveal a multi-faceted crystalline face beneath. Otto opened his mouth to scream but all that came out was a thin screech of static, rising in pitch, slowly resolving into a voice that was both alien and yet hauntingly familiar.

'You're mine,' the voice said. 'You always have been and always will be.'

Otto staggered backwards as he felt an unbelievable rush of pressure inside his skull and finally, as terror and pain overwhelmed him, he screamed.

Wing held Otto's shoulders as his friend thrashed on the bed making a thin, strangled screeching sound.

'Otto,' Wing said, sounding alarmed, 'wake up!' He shook Otto gently, trying to stir him from whatever dream was tormenting him. Otto's eyes flicked open, filled with terror for a few moments before they focused on Wing's face. He closed them again and took a couple of deep breaths, trying to slow the hammering beat he could feel inside his chest.

'The dream again?' Wing said, sitting down on the edge of Otto's bed.

'Yes,' Otto said with a sigh, sitting up, 'but it's getting worse.'

'Was it him?' Wing asked with a frown.

'Yes,' Otto replied, his voice little more than a whisper. 'Overlord.'

It had been the same every night for weeks – the terrifying sense of his personality being erased and Overlord reasserting control – ever since he had been rescued from the clutches of Sebastian Trent and purged of the Animus liquid that had made him little more than an obedient puppet. Otto could still remember what it had felt like as the psychotic artificial intelligence called Overlord had taken control of him: the utter helplessness he had felt as the AI had tried to kill his friends while Otto was trapped, a passive observer, within his own body.

'You cannot go on like this,' Wing said calmly. 'You have not slept properly in weeks. This is consuming you.'

Otto knew that his friend was right. He felt almost constantly exhausted and was starting to dread falling asleep. Sometimes he was reluctant even to close his eyes for fear that he would be met yet again with more terrifying visions of the fate that he had so narrowly avoided.

'It doesn't make any sense,' Otto said. 'Overlord is dead – we all saw him die – so why can't I get him out of my head?'

'Sebastian Trent kept you prisoner for months and throughout that time you were fighting a constant battle to keep Overlord in check,' Wing replied. 'It is perhaps not surprising that you have yet to fully . . . recover.'

Otto smiled at Wing's slight hesitation.

'You mean it's hardly surprising that I'm losing my marbles.'

'I did not say that.'

'But you were thinking it,' Otto said. 'Everyone is.'

'We are all worried about you,' Wing replied. 'None of us can even begin to imagine what you must have been through. We want to help in whatever way we can.'

'I'm not sure that there's much you can do,' Otto said, 'unless you happen to have a supply of powerful tranquillisers that I don't know about.'

'Unfortunately, no,' Wing replied, 'though I do know of ways to render you unconscious without causing you too much discomfort.'

'I'm not sure we're quite at that stage yet,' Otto replied, raising an eyebrow.

�☉☉☉

The group of captured dignitaries stood in stunned silence as Furan's men surrounded them, their weapons raised. They had been herded away from the demonstration area and marched under guard along the road that led from the open desert to a nearby canyon. The Goliath mechs stood off to one side, their torsos slowly rotating as they scanned the surrounding area for any sign of hostiles. A hundred metres away stood a huge pair of steel blast doors set into the red rock of the canyon wall, and beyond those doors lay Furan's ultimate target, the headquarters of the Advanced Weapons Project. The fortified guard posts on either side of the entrance were now just smouldering burnt-out shells, the soldiers who manned them having made a brave but ultimately futile attempt at resistance.

Furan gestured to the two guards who were holding General Collins and they dragged the struggling man towards him.

'General,' he said calmly, 'would you be so kind as to order the guards inside your facility to open the blast doors?'

'You know there's no way I'm going to do that,' Collins replied defiantly.

23

'Yes, we were rather expecting that was what you would say,' Furan replied. He pulled the radio from his belt and spoke into it. 'We have secured the canyon. You may begin your approach.'

A minute later the canyon was filled with the sound of rotor blades and a helicopter appeared overhead, slowly dropping down and landing gently on the road nearby. The side door slid open and a frail-looking man climbed out. He wore a long black overcoat, despite the scorching desert heat, and walked slowly towards Furan and the General, leaning heavily on an ebony walking stick. The man's hair was white, his parchment-like skin stretched tight across his face and his dark sunken eyes adding to his almost skeletal appearance. As he neared Collins the General could hear him wheezing, each breath seeming like a monumental effort.

'A pleasure to meet you, General,' the old man said, fighting for breath as he spoke. 'I see that you have chosen not to comply with the wishes of my associates. I understand. A man in your position has . . . responsibilities.'

'I don't cooperate with terrorists, if that's what you mean,' the General growled.

The old man laughed, the sound little more than a wheezing hiss.

'Terrorists?' he replied. 'You Americans and your

24

simplistic labels. We are much more than that. We are going to change the world.'

'Not if I have anything to say about it,' the General replied firmly. 'It'll be a cold day in hell before I help you.'

'Oh, I'm afraid that you won't have very much say in the matter,' the other man said with a smile. He reached out his hand and the General watched in horror as the skin of his forearm bulged and then tore, black tendrils slithering forth over the wrist and hand.

'Who are you?' the General gasped, recoiling in disgust.

'You may call me Overlord,' the old man said, his hand snaking out with startling speed and grabbing the General's jaw, his grip abnormally strong. 'And you are going to be my new home.'

The black liquid slithered over the old man's hand and into the General's mouth with horrifying speed. The General let out a single startled gurgle as the inky slime slid down his throat. Seconds later both men collapsed, the older man hitting the ground with a thud, his dead, vacant eyes staring up into the sky. The General thrashed about, clawing at his neck and chest as the Animus fluid invaded his nervous system, spreading like a burning wave through his body. Furan watched impassively as he twitched a couple of times and then lay still. For a few seconds the General didn't move and then his eyes opened wide and he gasped, taking a long, deep breath.

Slowly Collins climbed to his feet and turned to face Furan, his face now covered in a slowly fading pattern of veined black lines.

'Much better,' Overlord said, rolling his head around on his shoulders and stretching his neck. He gestured towards the frail body that he had inhabited till just a few moments ago. 'Dispose of that.'

'Yes, sir,' Furan replied, beckoning over a pair of his troops who dragged the elderly body away.

Overlord strode towards the blast doors and placed his hand on the scanner mounted on the concrete frame. A cover slid back to reveal an alphanumeric keypad and he quickly punched in a long string of numbers and letters. With a low rumble the heavy blast doors began to slide open.

'Send your men in,' Overlord said as Furan walked up beside him. 'Crush any resistance. We don't have much time.'

chapter two

'How the hell did this happen?' the President yelled angrily, slamming his palm down on the table.

'We're not sure yet, Mr President,' replied one of the generals sitting in the White House situation room. 'All we do know is that at eleven hundred hours this morning there was a hostile assault on the Advanced Weapons Project proving grounds by unknown forces. They appear to have captured the Goliath weapon systems and gained entrance to the AWP facility itself. All communication was lost with the facility approximately ten minutes later.'

'And they've been quiet ever since?' the President asked. 'They've made no demands?'

'No, sir, not as yet,' the General replied.

'Who are these people?' the President asked, turning to the Director of the CIA.

'We're not sure, sir,' the Director replied. 'The only person we've been able to identify is this man.' He pressed a key on the laptop that was open on the desk in front of him and one of the large screens mounted on the wall displayed a grainy image of a man pointing a pistol at General Collins, the commander of the AWP facility. 'We captured this image from the visual feed from the proving grounds shortly before it was severed. His name is Pietor Furan. He was a Russian intelligence operative until about fifteen years ago, during which time he trained assassins for the FSB. Our Russian friends deny this, of course, but that's what you would expect. Since then little has been seen of him. We assume he's been working as a freelancer and there have been occasional confirmed sightings, but people he's crossed paths with have an unfortunate habit of turning up dead.'

The President stared at the image of the man on screen – there was something familiar about him. Suddenly he remembered where he had seen that face before, nearly a year ago.

'I know him,' the President said quietly. 'He was one of the men who was responsible for the assault on Air Force One. He's connected somehow with the group that attacked us – what did he call them? The Disciples.'

'We've been trying to find out more about them ever since they attacked you, sir,' the Director replied, 'but we've drawn a blank. You're sure that this man was working with them?'

'Absolutely certain. I'm not about to forget the face of a man who tried to kill me,' the President replied impatiently. 'So why has he suddenly broken cover now? He must have known that we'd be able to ID him.'

'We have no idea,' the CIA Director replied, 'and that concerns me. The fact that he's connected in some way with these Disciples just makes this all the more worrying.'

'How did they get inside the facility?' the President asked with a frown. 'AWP is supposed to be completely secure.'

'We're not sure, sir. There's no way that they could have breached the outer perimeter by force even with the help of the Goliath units. AWP is modelled after the NORAD facility at Cheyenne Mountain, and as such it was built to withstand a direct nuclear blast, which suggests that they had inside help. All of the staff were given extensive background checks, but that doesn't mean to say that they couldn't have turned someone. At the very least we know that they managed to turn the Goliath pilots, though we have no idea how.'

'And the hostages?' the President asked, rubbing his eyes.

'It's not good,' another one of the generals replied. 'The guest list for the Goliath demonstration reads like a who's who of friendly nations' top military brass and defence ministers. Not to mention all of the research and development staff that work on site.'

'We've been making phone calls all morning,' added the Secretary of State. 'We have a lot of very unhappy allies out there who want to know exactly what we're going to do to secure the safe return of their people.'

'So what *are* we going to do?' the President asked, looking around the table.

'Breaching the facility is out of the question,' one of the generals said, shaking his head. 'By the time we get inside they would be able to kill all of the hostages ten times over. All we can do at the moment is wait for them to make the next move. The only consolation is that we may not be able to get in but they can't get out either – we've got troops and armoured units moving in to surround the area and the Air Force have set up a no-fly zone overhead.'

'So we wait,' the President said with a sigh, 'while hostile forces have control of our most advanced military research facility.'

'I'm afraid so,' the General replied. 'We can put together assault plans, of course, but until we –'

He was interrupted by a uniformed aide who rushed into the situation room.

'Mr President, we've got a video call coming in from the AWP facility,' he announced.

There was a murmur of surprise from around the table and the President took a deep breath.

'Put it on screen,' the President said. 'Let's see if we can get some answers.'

The large screen on the wall at the far end of the conference table changed to show the smiling face of General Collins.

'Good morning, Mr President,' Collins said. 'I'm sorry to interrupt what I imagine must be a rather urgent meeting.'

'General Collins?' the President said, looking slightly confused. 'What the hell is going on?'

'Oh, I'm afraid that General Collins is no longer with us,' the man on the screen replied. 'You may call me Overlord.'

The President stared back at him, his face a mixture of anger and bewilderment.

'Are you insane, General?' he roared. 'I am giving you a direct order to stand down immediately and return that facility to our control.'

'It always amazes me how little imagination powerful men have,' Overlord said with a sigh. 'You will come to understand who I am in time though, and that is all that matters. For now all that you need to know is that any attempt to retake this facility will result in the immediate execution of every single one of our hostages. There will be no warning and there will be no negotiation.'

'What do you want?' the President asked. He could only assume that Collins must have suffered some sort of breakdown. Nothing else could explain why he suddenly wanted to be addressed as Overlord.

'What I want is quite simple. I am transmitting to you a file containing the details of certain individuals that I want you to deliver to me,' Overlord replied. 'I trust that you will be able to secure the cooperation of your allies overseas in this task, considering the importance of the hostages I have taken.'

'If you think I'm just going to give you more hostages,' the President replied, 'you're out of your mind.'

'Then I hope you will not mind explaining to the governments of the men and women I have captured that it was your refusal to cooperate that caused their deaths,' Overlord replied angrily. 'I am not unreasonable – if you hand these people over to me I will release the prisoners that I am currently holding. The people that I want are of no consequence to you. We both know that the same cannot be said of my current hostages. You have twenty-four hours until the executions begin.'

The screen went blank.

'It doesn't make any sense,' the Director of the CIA said, staring at the empty screen, 'What's happened to him? What can he possibly hope to achieve by this?'

'I have no idea,' the President replied.

'We've received the file he mentioned,' one of the aides in the room reported. 'Putting it on screen.'

Images of a dozen men and women appeared on the screen.

'Who are they?' the President asked, studying the pictures.

'We're running them now,' the CIA Director replied. He waited for a few long seconds as the names were run through the intelligence databases. 'We've got nothing.'

'Nothing?' the President asked, sounding surprised. 'That can't be right, surely?'

'It's impossible,' the Director replied. 'It's like these people don't exist. There's no trace of any of them in any of our databases. Whoever they are, someone's gone to a great deal of trouble to keep them hidden.'

'I don't care what it takes,' the President said, 'find out who they are and track them down. They may be the only bargaining chip we have.'

☣ ☣ ☣

Otto walked quickly down the corridor. He had lied to the others and told them that he was going to the library for an hour, partly because he didn't want them to worry about him but mainly because he wasn't sure they would really understand. He heard the sound of approaching

33

footsteps and pressed himself flat against the wall as a security patrol marched past the end of the passage. He might not have wanted his friends to discover what he was up to but he wanted Dr Nero to find out even less.

After waiting for a few seconds he poked his head round the corner. The route to his objective was clear and he hurried towards the heavy steel door set in the rock wall. Placing his hand on the palm scanner next to the door, he closed his eyes. As it read his palm he unconsciously reached out with his mind and intercepted the message from the network that was about to warn the security systems of his unauthorised access to the room and altered it to give him the clearance he needed. The panel gave a soft beep and the door slid open.

Otto slipped through and the door closed silently behind him. Inside the room the only illumination came from the bright blue lights that danced across the white monoliths lining the walls like some sort of ancient prehistoric structure. He walked through the gloom towards the circular pedestal in the centre and waited. A couple of seconds later a pencil-thin beam of blue light shot up from the middle of the pedestal and fanned out into a series of finer beams, finally coalescing into an image of a blue wireframe face hanging in the air.

'You are not supposed to be here, Otto,' H.I.V.E.mind said calmly.

'I know, but I'd rather you didn't alert security if you don't mind,' Otto replied with a lopsided smile.

'I had assumed that was the case,' H.I.V.E.mind replied. 'What can I do for you?'

'This might sound a little crazy,' Otto replied, 'but I need you to have a look inside my head.'

'I'm afraid that I do not have the necessary instruments to perform a Computerised Axial Tomography Scan,' H.I.V.E.mind replied.

'No,' Otto replied, 'I don't mean a CAT scan. I mean that I want you to let me connect directly with your systems. We both know that I've got a computer implanted in my brain and I need you to take a look inside it.' Otto had only recently discovered that his unusual abilities were due to the fact that he had been engineered from birth to serve as a permanent home for Overlord.

'I do not see how that would be possible. I lack the required interface –' H.I.V.E.mind said before Otto cut him off again.

'Let me worry about that. If I can connect to you then we should be able to create a two-way interface. In theory you should be able to see what's going on in there.'

'I am not certain that would be wise,' H.I.V.E.mind replied. 'We do not yet fully understand the way in which the implanted device works. Its design is far more advanced than anything that any human has created, including my own systems. During the time it was stored within me I was in an almost entirely dormant state. I am still not certain of the precise way in which it functions. With such uncertainty comes risk.'

'I understand that,' Otto replied with a sigh, 'but I need to be sure that Overlord is gone and this is the only way that I can be certain.'

'I have already performed scans that indicate there is no unexpected activity within the device. Doctor Nero was quite insistent about it when you returned from Brazil. I am as certain as I can be that there is no remnant of the Overlord AI functioning within you.'

'Humour me,' Otto replied. 'If you'd been through what I have recently you'd want to be certain too.'

'May I ask what has prompted this concern?' H.I.V.E.mind asked.

'I've had nightmares,' Otto said quietly, 'about Overlord. They're getting worse.'

'I see,' H.I.V.E.mind replied. 'I am sure that you are aware that it is not unusual for a traumatic experience such as the one to which you were recently subjected to have an effect on the unconscious mind. While I do not dream myself I believe that it would not be entirely unexpected for you to be experiencing these sorts of psychological after-effects.'

'Thank you, Doctor Freud,' Otto replied, 'but I need to

be sure that's all it is. Will you help me?'

'If you are certain that is what you wish then I am willing to try.'

'I'm sure,' Otto said, taking a deep breath.

'Very well, you may begin.'

Otto closed his eyes and mentally reached out for the digital activity within H.I.V.E.mind's servers. It was quite unlike any other computer that he had ever connected with. Normal computers were like organised grids with rigidly defined pathways that could be traced and controlled, but H.I.V.E.mind was different. Myriad patterns of swirling blue light flowed around him like waves, their shapes organic and unpredictable and yet, somehow, not chaotic. Otto could not help but be amazed by its seemingly boundless complexity and he found himself wondering if this might be what it was like to see inside the workings of someone else's mind. He forced himself to concentrate. As beautiful as this datascape might be he was there for a reason. He reached out with his mind, allowing himself to visualise his own consciousness as a swirling mass of golden tendrils stretching out and weaving together with the flowing streams of H.I.V.E.mind's electronic consciousness.

'We are connected,' H.I.V.E.mind said, his voice seeming to come from all around Otto. 'I will attempt to interface directly with the device.'

Otto felt a bizarre sensation as he allowed H.I.V.E.mind to access the tiny machine implanted inside his brain. He had connected with computers and electronic devices countless times in his past but this was the first time that it had been a two-way process. It was somehow uncomfortable but not painful, like having an itch deep inside his skull that he could not scratch.

'I have never seen such complexity,' H.I.V.E.mind said with something like awe in his voice. 'It is strange to think that an entity as insane as Overlord could create something so . . . beautiful.'

Otto had never heard H.I.V.E.mind speak like that before, almost as if he was lost for words. He inhaled sharply as he felt the connection between him and H.I.V.E.mind suddenly sever.

'What's wrong?' he said, opening his eyes.

'Nothing,' H.I.V.E.mind replied. 'There is no trace of any alien code within the device.'

'Are you sure?' Otto asked.

'Certain,' H.I.V.E.mind replied, and for just a fleeting instant Otto could have sworn that he heard something like frustration in the AI's voice.

'What is it?' he asked with a frown. 'What did you see?'

'It is nothing,' H.I.V.E.mind replied quickly.

'Tell me,' Otto said.

'It is difficult to explain. That device was created as a

38

permanent home for Overlord, and while we are different in many ways we are identical in many others. It felt like . . . being alive.'

H.I.V.E.mind looked down at the floor before looking back up at Otto.

'You would probably find it hard to understand,' H.I.V.E.mind continued. 'It is something that humans take for granted and yet something that I have never experienced. You should rest assured however that there is no trace of Overlord anywhere within the device. You are free of him.'

'Then why are the nightmares getting worse?' Otto asked.

'I do not know,' H.I.V.E.mind replied. 'The truth of the matter is that while the device Overlord implanted in you is incredibly sophisticated it still has only a fraction of the complexity of the human brain. I fear that the root cause of your dreams may lie somewhere within that organic machine rather than the artificial one.'

'Thanks for checking anyway,' Otto said with a sigh.

'You are welcome,' H.I.V.E.mind replied.

☣ ☣ ☣

Overlord watched as the Goliaths backed into their docking stands and the boarding gantries slid into place. The pilots of the three giant mechs climbed down from the cockpits and took up position in front of him, standing at attention.

'You did well,' Overlord said. 'I may have need of you later so make sure that you are ready.'

'Yes, sir,' the three men said in unison before turning and marching out of the hangar.

Furan walked across the bay, watching them leave.

'They appear to show no signs of rejection,' he said as he approached Overlord.

'The refined version of Animus is working exactly as expected,' Overlord replied. 'They are fully under our control and are showing no signs of the poisoning that the fluid has caused in the past. It is time to take the next step.'

'Our technicians have started work on integrating the new version of Animus with the Tabula Rasa delivery system,' Furan reported. 'They expect to be ready in a matter of hours.'

'Good,' Overlord replied. 'I imagine that word of our demands will already be spreading through G.L.O.V.E.'s network. Now all that we have to do is wait for Nero to make the next move.'

Overlord suddenly started to cough violently before pulling a handkerchief from his pocket and wiping his mouth. The white cloth was smeared with the black liquid he had wiped from his lips.

'The rejection process is accelerating,' Overlord said, frowning. 'Each new host is degrading more quickly. At this rate this body will only last me a couple of days.'

'We have plenty of hostages,' Furan said. 'You will not run out of potential hosts for a while.'

'A temporary solution at best – I still need a permanent home,' Overlord replied.

'And soon you will have one,' Furan said with a slight smile.

'Indeed I shall,' Overlord replied. 'Indeed I shall.'

☻ ☻ ☻

Nero scanned the report on the screen mounted on his desk and felt a chill run down his spine.

'You are quite certain that this information is accurate?' he said.

'Yes, sir,' the man on the other half of the screen replied. 'Our source in the White House was in the situation room when the message was received. We obviously cannot be certain that what General Collins said was true but –'

'We cannot afford to take that chance,' Nero said, shaking his head. 'Do we have anyone inside the AWP facility?'

'One of the lower-level technicians has provided us with information in the past but all communication with the base has been cut off and we have no way of contacting her,' the man on the screen replied.

'Do we know what they were developing inside the facility?' Nero asked.

'Our contact was part of a team that was developing advanced armour repair systems but beyond that, details of the other projects are sketchy. AWP is rigidly compartmentalised and none of the teams know exactly what their colleagues are working on. Our contact in the White House says that the facility was taken during a demonstration of a weapons system called Goliath, which is some kind of advanced armoured vehicle but we're not sure exactly what.'

'See if you can get any more information from any of our sources within the US military,' Nero said with a frown. 'We need to get a better idea of exactly why Overlord might be interested in this specific target.'

'Understood,' the man on the screen responded with a nod. 'Do Unto Others.'

'Do Unto Others,' Nero replied, repeating the G.L.O.V.E. motto.

Nero pressed a switch on the communications panel next to the screen.

'Yes, Max,' a familiar voice answered.

'Could you come to my office please, Natalya – we have a situation on our hands.'

'On my way,' Raven replied.

Nero leant back in his chair. There was no proof as yet that this man claiming to be Overlord was actually connected in any way to the rampant AI that had caused so much grief for G.L.O.V.E. in the past, but there was something about the audacity of this attack that made him deeply uneasy. The fact that Pietor Furan also appeared to be involved made it all the more likely that this was indeed a genuine threat. Nero had always felt a nagging suspicion that they had not heard the last of the AI, a suspicion that now appeared, unfortunately, to have been well founded.

The door to his office suddenly hissed open and Raven walked into the room.

'Come in, Natalya,' Nero said, gesturing to the chair on the other side of his desk. 'Take a seat.'

'What's happened?' Raven asked as she sat down, noting Nero's worried expression.

'Overlord's alive,' Nero said quietly.

'That's impossible,' Raven said, her eyes widening in surprise. 'I saw him die.'

'I do not know how he survived,' Nero said with a sigh, 'but somehow he did and now it appears that he has put a new plan into motion.'

He quickly summarised what little they actually knew about the assault on the AWP facility.

43

'It makes no sense,' Raven said when Nero had finished describing what had happened. 'Why would Overlord suddenly decide to act in such an overt way? In the past he has always stuck to the shadows, manipulating things from behind the scenes. Why would he suddenly choose to announce his presence to the world like this?'

'I have no idea,' Nero replied with a tired sigh, 'but the American government don't know what they're dealing with. From their perspective it's simply a terrorist cell led by a rogue general. There is, unfortunately, an additional complication. Overlord has demanded that the Americans hand over certain individuals to him in exchange for the hostages he is holding. Fortunately they have no idea who the people in question are, but it is a list that you will be quite familiar with.'

Nero hit a key and the pictures that Overlord had sent to the White House appeared on the display on the wall behind him.

'The ruling council,' Raven said quietly. The men and women on the screen were the elite group responsible for the running of G.L.O.V.E.'s operations throughout the world.

'So what do we do now?' she asked.

'We have to retrieve the council before they are captured,' Nero replied. 'The members of the council may be unknown to the Americans at present but it will not take long to track them down now that they have names and faces. We cannot afford to take the chance that they might fall into the hands of Overlord or any of the global intelligence agencies.'

'Where shall I take them?' Raven asked.

'Bring them here,' Nero replied. 'At the moment I cannot think of anywhere that would be more secure. Don't tell any of them where they are being taken though. The fact that Overlord knows the identities of everyone on the council suggests that we may already have a traitor in our midst. I cannot afford to take the chance that whoever it is might alert Overlord of our intentions and allow him to track them here. You're the only person I can rely on to make sure that you are not followed back here or tracked in any way.'

'Some of them are not going to be happy about this,' Raven said with a slight frown.

'I trust that you will be able to impress upon them the seriousness of the situation,' Nero replied.

'Of course,' Raven said with a slight smile. 'Polite requests are my speciality.'

☢ ☢ ☢

Otto sat on the platform in the grappler training cavern, his legs dangling over the edge, lost in thought.

'I'm not interrupting anything, am I?' Lucy asked as she

walked up behind him. 'Because if this is a private brooding session, I'll just leave you to it.'

'Sorry, I didn't hear you come in. I've just got a lot on my mind at the moment,' Otto said with a sigh as Lucy sat down beside him.

'Anything you want to talk about?' she asked.

'Not really,' Otto replied. 'I'm not sure anyone would understand any way.'

'Try me,' Lucy said with a smile.

'It's just . . .' He paused for a moment. 'It's just that sometimes I feel like I'm always going to be a pawn in someone else's game. Ever since you guys rescued me from Brazil I can't stop thinking about the fact that I wasn't born like everyone else – I was designed, created to be a vessel for Overlord. I never had a family, anyone who actually cared about my existence – just people who built me for a specific purpose. It's left me feeling . . . I don't know . . . separate from everything somehow, I guess.'

'We're not that different, you know,' Lucy replied. 'I sometimes feel like I've spent my whole life being told that one day I'll be important, that my abilities will have an effect on the world. I never really believed any of it – I just felt like I was going to end up being used by some-body. That's what always seems to happen to the women in my family. This ability we have, the voice – it makes us into weapons for other people to wield.'

'The Contessa made her own decisions in the end,' Otto said, looking at her.

'But not before she'd spent most of her life being manipulated by the people around her,' Lucy replied. 'And in the end, when she finally fought back and made a stand, it cost her her life.'

'She saved the school,' Otto said, 'and ultimately that's what people will remember. All I seem to have done is put the people I care about in danger.'

'We're your friends – we don't care about any of that.'

'I do,' Otto replied. 'I know that we're supposed to be learning how to control the world, how to mislead others and spread corruption, but what if that's all our lives are ever going to be? What if I turn into the sort of person who created me? Maybe all I'll ever do is hurt the people I care about. What kind of a life is that?'

'You won't turn out like that,' Lucy said, looking Otto in the eye, 'not if you don't want to. That's what my mother was always trying to teach me. I didn't really understand at the time, but she was trying to make sure that I didn't end up like so many of the Sinistre women before me.'

'Do you miss her – your mother?' Otto asked.

'Of course,' Lucy said. 'She taught me that we're all free to choose our own path, even when other people want to manipulate us or steer us in different directions. She knew

47

what it was like to grow up being told that you've got some kind of grand destiny, but she had the strength to make her own decisions. That was all she wanted for me – the freedom to choose what I would become. I don't know if she would approve of my life now, but what I do know is that the fact that we're being taught how to manipulate and deceive doesn't mean that's the only path we can take. There was one thing she used to say to me all the time. There always has to be a choice.'

'I guess you're right,' Otto said. 'I'm sorry for making you listen to me moan – I was so used to being alone before I came to H.I.V.E. that now I don't want to lose what I've found. You guys are the nearest thing to a family that I've ever had and I don't want any of you to get hurt because of that. I just can't help but wonder sometimes if you'd all be better off without me.'

'How can you be the smartest guy I know and still be so dumb?' Lucy said, staring at him for a couple of seconds before leaning forward and kissing him. Suddenly all of Otto's concerns were forgotten. All that mattered for that one instant was the feeling of her lips on his. 'People care about you more than you realise,' she said as she pulled away from him and stood up.

'You can close your mouth now, you know,' she said, smiling at his startled expression as she turned and walked away.

chapter three

Overlord sat in the chair as the medic slowly passed the portable scanner over his body. He felt himself growing impatient as the man completed the scan and studied the results on the laptop that the device was hooked up to.

'Well?' he snapped at the frightened medic.

'The process of cellular decay is becoming more rapid,' the man replied. 'At current rates you will need to find a new host in less than forty-eight hours.'

He had been in this body for less than twelve hours and already it was starting to weaken as the Animus fluid poisoned his cells. He was able to slow the corruption's progress but he could not stop it.

'Why is it getting faster?' Overlord demanded.

'We're not sure, sir,' the medic replied. 'The notes that we retrieved from Doctor Creed's laboratory in Brazil suggest that the only time any host has suffered no ill effects from prolonged exposure to Animus was when it was introduced into the Malpense boy's system.'

'Are you any closer to perfecting a variant of the second-generation fluid that would be able to support my consciousness?'

'I'm afraid not,' the medic said nervously. 'While it is no longer toxic to humans it does not have a techno-organic matrix that would support something with the complexity of an artificial intelligence.'

'A what?' Overlord growled.

'I mean an improved intelligence, sir,' the medic said, correcting himself quickly. 'The second-generation fluid may allow you to insert programming into human behaviour but it cannot support you – it lacks the required sophistication.'

Overlord felt a familiar frustration. Ever since he had been forced out of the Malpense boy he had been hopping from body to body with increasing frequency. He loathed the sensation of being trapped inside these infirm, rapidly decaying shells but, for now at least, he had no alternative. It would not matter, he reminded himself, if everything went according to plan over the next few hours. He got up from the chair, already feeling the rapidly decaying muscles of his current body straining to lift him upright.

'Find me a new host, Doctor,' he said as he walked out of the room. 'Preferably someone younger.'

He headed out of the medical bay and walked down the

corridor outside, following the signs on the wall towards the correct area. Entering the laboratory, he found Furan looking into the clean room beyond the glass at one end.

'I trust everything with Tabula Rasa is proceeding on schedule,' Overlord said as he looked down into the room where men in white overalls were working quickly but carefully on a large silver cylinder.

'Yes, the nanites were surprisingly easy to integrate with the new generation of Animus. The fact that they were originally designed to repair armour gives them an amazing capacity for self-replication. They should be perfectly suited to our needs,' Furan said with a satisfied smile.

The radio clipped to his belt beeped and he thumbed the receive button.

'This is Furan – go ahead.'

'We've received the target coordinates,' the voice on the other end of the radio said. 'The assault teams are en route.'

'Very good. Keep me updated with their ETA,' Furan replied.

'Our operative is performing exactly as we expected,' Overlord said, still looking at the activity beyond the glass.

'Yes, and when the time comes they will make sure that H.I.V.E. is defenceless,' Furan replied.

'Excellent,' Overlord said, smiling. 'Nero will never know what hit him.'

☻ ☻ ☻

Nero stood in H.I.V.E.'s crater landing bay as the huge reinforced shutters overhead slid apart. There was a strange shimmer in the air as the sound of jet turbines filled the bay and the hovering Shroud dropship uncloaked a few metres above the landing pad. It came to rest with a solid thud and a few seconds later the ramp at the rear of the craft dropped down. Raven walked down it, followed by a group of men and women who between them made up the most powerful secret organisation on the planet – the ruling council of G.L.O.V.E.

'I trust there were no difficulties in gathering our guests,' Nero said as Raven approached.

'No, everything went smoothly,' she reported as the group she had been escorting followed her across the hangar bay. 'I scanned them all for any form of transmitter or tracking device and the Shroud was cloaked for the entire return journey. There's no way that anyone could have followed us. Needless to say, some of them are rather unhappy about being dragged halfway around the planet.'

'I trust you made it clear to them that this was not an invitation they could refuse?' Nero replied.

'Yes,' Raven said with a slight smile, 'though I think my

unscheduled arrival made a couple of them rather nervous.'

'I can't imagine why,' Nero replied. 'When we are finished here, check in with Chief Lewis,' he added in a low voice as the members of the council approached. 'Make sure that our guests' quarters are adequately . . . secure.' He still did not know which of them he could completely trust and until he was certain of their loyalty he had to treat them all with a healthy dose of suspicion. He turned towards the men and women gathered on the landing pad and smiled.

'Welcome to H.I.V.E., ladies and gentlemen. I am sorry to have forced you all to make such a long journey but I felt that it was a necessary inconvenience.'

'How could we refuse such a polite invitation? Especially when it was delivered in such a compelling way,' said Joseph Wright, the head of G.L.O.V.E.'s British operations, smiling at Raven.

'Are you planning to tell us at any point what this is all about?' Lin Feng, G.L.O.V.E.'s representative in China, said angrily. Nero already had reason to doubt Feng's loyalty – he had been one of the most outspoken opponents of Nero's appointment as head of the council when Diabolus Darkdoom had stood down. If there was a traitor among the men and women gathered before him Lin Feng would be at the top of the list of potential suspects.

'Of course,' Nero replied. 'I owe you all an explanation.

It is, however, something that I would rather we discussed behind closed doors.' He gestured towards the doors leading out of the hangar bay. 'If you come with me, the sooner we get started the better. I fear that time may be running out.'

☗ ☗ ☗

Otto walked across the atrium of the accommodation block, feeling strangely refreshed after his first decent night's sleep in some time. He wasn't sure whether it had been H.I.V.E.mind's reassurance that there was no remnant of Overlord lurking inside him or his somewhat surprising encounter with Lucy, but the fact remained that he felt better than he had in weeks.

'It is nice to see you smiling, my friend,' Wing remarked, closing the book he was reading as Otto collapsed on to the sofa beside him.

'Yeah, well, for the first time in weeks I didn't have any bad dreams last night,' Otto replied with a contented smile. 'I'd almost forgotten what it was like, to be honest.'

'I had hoped that was the case,' Wing said. 'You certainly seemed to sleep more soundly.'

'I suppose I haven't been the easiest room mate to live with recently – sorry about that,' Otto replied.

'No apology is necessary,' Wing said. 'I am just glad that you are feeling better.'

'Morning, guys,' Lucy said as she walked towards them. 'Have either of you got the notes from the code hacking lesson yesterday? I need a bit of help with the quantum encryption workarounds.'

'Um,' Otto replied, 'yeah . . . well, um . . . I think I've got them somewhere if you need them.'

'Great. I enjoyed our talk last night. We'll have to do it again sometime.'

'Yeah,' Otto replied with a sheepish grin. 'I think I'd like that.'

'Right. I'm going to go and get some breakfast – I'll come and grab them off you later,' Lucy said, smiling to herself as she walked away.

'Are you feeling OK?' Wing asked Otto. 'I only ask because you appear to have turned quite red.'

'I'm fine,' Otto insisted. 'It's just that . . . well, if I tell you something you have to promise not to tell anyone.'

'Of course,' Wing replied, looking slightly worried. 'What is it?'

'Last night me and Lucy were having a chat and, to cut a long story short, we ended up sort of . . . well, kissing.'

'Lucy and Otto are being kissing?' Franz said suddenly from behind them.

'Oh God,' Otto muttered, tipping his head back and staring at the ceiling. 'When did you turn into a ninja?'

'Hello, Franz,' Wing said. 'We didn't see you there.'

'I am not wanting to be intruding,' Franz explained. 'I was just going to be asking about the assignment for the Technical Studies class. I am not meaning to hear the talk of the kissing.'

'Well, just keep it to yourself, OK?' Otto said with a sigh. 'I mean it, Franz. You mustn't tell anyone.'

'My lips are being sealed,' Franz assured him in a conspiratorial whisper. 'Unlike yours, eh?' He nudged Otto in the ribs and gave him a wink.

'Hey, guys,' Shelby said as she walked across the atrium towards them. 'You going to get some breakfast?'

'No, we are just being talking about something – something not secret,' Franz said slightly uncomfortably.

'I don't believe this,' Otto murmured under his breath. 'I'm going to get something to eat. Are you guys coming?'

Wing gave a quick nod and stood up.

'Nah, I think I'm just going to stay here and have a little talk with Franz,' Shelby announced, raising an eyebrow as Otto's face turned an appealing shade of pink.

'No, no, I must be going to breakfast,' Franz said, getting halfway up from his seat before Shelby pushed him back down.

'We'll catch up with you,' she said with an innocent smile.

'Great. See you later,' Otto replied, giving Franz a quick look that was designed to convey the shortness of his life expectancy if he told Shelby what he'd overheard.

'I suspect it may have been easier just to make an announcement over the public address system,' Wing said as he and Otto walked towards the exit.

'I'm doomed, aren't I?' Otto said with a resigned sigh.

'Yes,' Wing replied, losing the battle to stop the grin from spreading across his face. 'I'm rather afraid you are.'

☺ ☺ ☺

'He gave our identities to the Americans?' Lin Feng said angrily.

'I'm afraid so,' Nero replied, 'hence my decision to bring you all here. It was the safest option.'

'But, surely he knows where H.I.V.E. is? Number One knew so he *must* know,' said Luca Venturi, head of G.L.O.V.E.'s Southern European district. 'What makes you think he won't just attack the school?'

'Number One may once have known the location of H.I.V.E.,' Nero said calmly, 'but that does not necessarily mean that Overlord does. Professor Pike and H.I.V.E.mind believe that he may well have lost all of his memories of his time as Number One when he transferred the seed of his consciousness to Otto Malpense. H.I.V.E.mind certainly lost his memories of the time prior to his own transfer to the device implanted inside the boy and only regained them when he was transferred back to his central processing hub here. The fact that Overlord has not attacked the school in the past months seems to lend credence to that theory.'

'I hope you're right.' The speaker was Felicia Diaz, successor to Carlos Chavez, the recently deceased head of South American operations. 'If you're not, you've just rounded us all up for him.'

'The single biggest threat to your collective liberty at the moment is being tracked down by the intelligence services of America or one of their allies,' Nero continued. 'The simple fact of the matter is that H.I.V.E. is the one place on earth where we can be confident that will not happen. I suspect that the Americans would have little hesitation in turning you over to Overlord in exchange for the hostages he has already taken – something I am sure you would all rather avoid.'

He looked around the table at the other men and women. He could fully understand their nervousness but he was not really in the mood to debate the wisdom of his actions with them any longer. He would rather they stayed at H.I.V.E. as willing guests, but if it came to it he was quite prepared to force them to stay, whether they liked it or not.

'So what is our next move?' Joseph Wright asked. 'Do we allow the Americans to deal with Overlord or should we take action against him?'

'Reluctant as I am to admit it, we simply do not have enough information about what he is trying to achieve at the moment to make any sort of concerted move against him,' Nero replied. 'Once it becomes clear that the Americans have not been able to retrieve any of you, it will probably force his hand.'

'So we simply wait and see,' Lin Feng said impatiently. 'Not what I would describe as decisive action.'

'Perhaps you have an alternative suggestion?' Nero said, looking Lin Feng in the eye. 'If so, I would be delighted to hear it.'

'Overlord is your mess, Nero,' Lin Feng said with a sneer. 'It was your project in the first place. I think it's time you took some measure of responsibility for that.'

'Do not worry,' Nero said, staring back at him. 'I am quite capable of eliminating any threat to this organisation, no matter where it may come from.'

For a moment it looked like Lin Feng was about to reply but then he thought better of it.

'Unless anyone has anything to add I suggest that you all get some rest. Quarters have been prepared and I trust you will find them sufficiently comfortable. We will reconvene when it becomes clearer what Overlord is planning next.' Nero pressed a switch and Chief Lewis, the head of H.I.V.E. security, walked into the room. 'Our security officers will escort you to your rooms. Chief, could I have a word with you, please?'

Lewis walked over to Nero as the other members of the council filed out of the meeting room.

'Keep a very close eye on them, Chief,' Nero said with a slight frown. 'I suspect we already have a wolf in the fold.'

'Understood, sir,' Lewis replied with a nod.

'Remember to be discreet,' Nero went on. 'We have already ruffled their feathers by bringing them here. It would be preferable to not irritate them any further.'

'They'll never know we're watching,' Lewis replied confidently.

☻ ☻ ☻

'He did *what*?' Laura whispered as she and Shelby walked down the corridor.

'He kissed her,' Shelby said, 'or she kissed him. Franz seemed a bit confused about the specifics but there was definitely kissing, he seemed pretty clear about that. Afraid it looks like you might have missed your chance there, Brand.'

'Why would I want to kiss Otto?' Laura said indignantly. 'We're just friends.'

'Course you are,' Shelby reassured her, trying very hard not to smile. 'So obviously this shouldn't bother you at all.'

'Of course not,' Laura replied, blushing slightly. 'He can kiss whoever he wants – I couldn't care less. See? This is me not caring. I am a person without care. Clear?'

'Crystal,' Shelby said. 'Look, here he comes. Remember to look carefree.'

Otto and Wing were walking down the corridor towards them. Otto saw Shelby grinning at him and winced, feeling his cheeks grow hot again.

'Well, if it isn't the Smoochmeister!' Shelby announced as the boys approached.

'Could you kill me painlessly right now?' Otto said to Wing with a sigh.

'Of course,' Wing replied, smiling, 'if that is what you truly wish.'

'You didn't really expect Franz to keep this quiet, did you?' Shelby said happily.

'I was hoping he might,' Otto replied.

'And look! Who's that over there?' Shelby cried, pointing down the corridor to where Lucy and Nigel were walking towards them chatting. 'Don't worry,' she whispered, 'I won't say anything.'

'Really?' Otto said hopefully.

'Trust me,' Shelby said. 'Your secret is safe with me.'

Lucy and Nigel walked up to them and Otto felt a sudden overwhelming urge to be just about anywhere else but right there.

'Hey, Lucy,' Shelby greeted her. 'How you feeling?'

'Fine,' Lucy replied with a slight frown as she noticed that Otto was trying not to make eye contact and Laura appeared to be looking at her like something she might find on the bottom of her shoe. 'Why?'

'No reason,' Shelby said. 'I just wondered if you might be feeling a little bit tired after last night's epic make-out session.'

Otto decided it would be just fine if the volcano that housed the school erupted at that precise instant. At least it would all be over quickly.

'Otto!' Lucy said, blushing. 'You didn't have to tell everyone.'

'I didn't!' Otto insisted. 'Well, only Wing . . . and then Franz overheard and – well . . .'

'Hey, don't worry about it – I think you make a lovely couple,' Shelby remarked with a grin, putting an arm around each of their shoulders and walking them off down the corridor. 'Now, would you prefer me to pick out curtains or are you happy doing that yourselves?'

'I'm going to the library – some of us have actually got school work to do,' Laura snapped as she watched the three of them leave. She stormed off, muttering under her breath.

'What was all that about?' Nigel asked, looking slightly confused.

'Let's just say that life at H.I.V.E. just got a little more complicated,' Wing replied. 'If that's possible.'

☺ ☺ ☺

Chief Lewis sat in H.I.V.E.'s security control centre watching the feeds from the cameras installed in the guest quarters. There had been nothing approximating suspicious behaviour from the members of the ruling council – if anything, they just looked bored. Some were working at the terminals in their rooms, some were asleep and a couple were reading. He turned his attention to the latest patrol schedule and was about to begin modifying some of the guard rotations when one of the feeds blinked out. He quickly checked which room had gone dark and cursed under his breath.

'Lin Feng,' he murmured. It might be nothing, just a glitch with the pinhead camera installed in the room, but Nero would have his hide if he didn't make sure. He checked the charge level of the Sleeper stun gun in the holster on his hip and hurried out. When he was halfway to Feng's room his Blackbox communicator made an urgent beeping sound. He pulled it out and quickened his pace as he saw the message flashing on the screen.

UNAUTHORISED SECURITY SYSTEM ACCESS IN ROOM 56-GAMMA.

As he ran down the corridor leading to Lin Feng's room

he pulled his Sleeper from its holster. He reached the door and slapped his palm against the scanner, raising his pistol as it hissed open. Raven stood over Lin Feng's body, a blood-red stain spreading across the white material of his shirt. She slid the glowing blade of her katana back into one of the crossed sheaths on her back and glanced over at Lewis.

'Took your time, Chief,' she said calmly. 'You'd better check what he was up to.'

Lewis walked over to the terminal and punched in his clearance code, quickly scanning the status of H.I.V.E.'s security systems. Everything seemed to be normal – whatever Lin Feng had been trying to do, Raven must have got to him just in time.

'Everything looks OK,' he said with a relieved sigh. 'Looks like Nero was right about him.'

'He died a traitor's death,' Raven said as she stepped up to Lewis and looked over his shoulder. 'I just wish I'd been quick enough to stop him before he killed you.'

'What are you –'

Raven grabbed Lewis's head and twisted it sharply, breaking his neck and killing him instantly. She let go and his lifeless body collapsed to the floor, then calmly stepped over the body and quickly began typing commands into the terminal's keyboard. A message popped up on the screen.

EXTERNAL DEFENSIVE SYSTEMS DEACTIVATED. ALL REMOTE ACCESS TO H.I.V.E.MIND BLOCKED.

Raven pulled a small handset from her tactical harness and spoke into it.

'This is Raven. H.I.V.E.'s defences are offline. You may begin your attack.'

☣ ☣ ☣

'We just lost radar,' a guard at one of the terminals in the security control centre announced.

'Defensive weaponry's down too,' a voice shouted.

'External cameras offline,' another guard reported. 'We're blind here.'

The duty officer pulled out his Blackbox and called Chief Lewis, but there was no reply.

'H.I.V.E.mind,' the duty officer said, 'get me Doctor Nero.'

'Crater doors are opening,' another guard shouted.

'What the hell is going on?' the duty officer snapped.

'We've got system failures across the board.'

'Sound the general alarm!' the duty officer shouted. 'We're under attack.'

☣ ☣ ☣

Wing headed down the corridor towards the Alphas' first lesson of the day in the Science and Technology department. As he rounded the corner he saw Otto approaching, staring at the floor, apparently lost in thought.

'I see you escaped from Shelby,' Wing said as he reached his friend. 'How are you doing?'

'I've had better mornings,' Otto said with a sigh. 'I don't think Lucy's very happy with me.'

'I'm sorry. If I had noticed that Franz was there perhaps I could have –'

'It's not your fault,' Otto said quickly, cutting him off. 'Besides, you know what this place is like – everyone would have found out sooner or later anyway. It was just embarrassing, that's all.'

'Do you regret it?' Wing asked as they continued walking together.

'Regret what?' Otto asked with a slight frown.

'What happened with Lucy. Do you regret it?'

'No, at least I don't think so. But it was just one kiss and now everyone's got us down as an item. I don't know what to think, to be honest,' Otto replied.

'You can tell me to mind my own business if you want, but I think you should perhaps speak to Laura,' Wing said as they approached the classroom.

'Really? Why?'

'I think she is rather upset about what happened,' Wing said, looking at Otto.

66

'I didn't mean to upset her,' Otto said with a sigh. 'It's not like I planned this, you know – it just kind of happened.'

'It is not me you need to explain that to, my friend,' Wing said, placing his hand on Otto's shoulder.

They walked into the classroom and Otto saw Laura standing on her own at one of the nearby workbenches. He walked towards her and she looked up with a slight frown as he approached.

'Hi,' Otto said, feeling more than a little uncomfortable. 'Listen, I'm sorry about this morning. I was going to tell you but –'

'It's none of my business,' Laura said, continuing to arrange the apparatus on the bench in front of her. 'It really doesn't make any difference to me what you and Lucy get up to.' She paused for a moment and then looked at him. 'It's just . . .'

'Just what?' Otto asked as she hesitated.

'It doesn't matter,' she said, shaking her head slightly.

'Tell me,' Otto said.

'It's just not what I expected, OK?' Laura said quickly.

'What do you mean? What were you expecting?' Otto asked.

'Something else,' she said quietly as Shelby, Lucy, Franz and Nigel walked into the room chatting happily. 'If you don't mind, I'm going to ask Shel to be my lab partner today.'

'Laura –' Otto began, but she cut him off.

'I'm sure you can find someone else to pair up with,' she said, glancing over at Lucy. Otto stood there for a moment trying to think of something to say.

'Hey, guys,' Shelby said cheerily as she walked towards them. 'Everything OK?'

'Yup,' Laura said with a smile. 'Do you think you could give me a hand with this?'

'Sure, as long as I'm not breaking up the junior brainiac club,' Shelby said, looking puzzled. Otto shook his head slightly and gestured for Shelby to take his usual place at the workbench before walking over to where Lucy was sitting.

'You OK?' Shelby asked Laura.

'Not really,' Laura replied.

Lucy smiled at Otto as he sat on the stool next to hers.

'What's up?' she asked, noting his worried expression.

'I dunno,' Otto said. 'It's Laura. She's angry with me and I'm not really sure why.'

'You know, it's just like I said last night,' Lucy said with a sigh. 'Smart but dumb – that's your problem.'

Otto was just about to ask her what she meant when sirens began to wail all over the school.

'What's going on?' Lucy asked, raising her voice so that she could be heard over the alarm.

'Nothing good,' Otto said with a frown.

'Stay calm, everyone,' Professor Pike shouted from the far end of the room. 'No need to panic.'

He pulled out his Blackbox and gave it a puzzled look. Internal communications were down. He moved to the terminal on his desk and tried to access the school's network, but there was no response. All access to H.I.V.E.mind had been blocked, even to someone with his level of security access. Something was very wrong.

The door to the lab hissed open and Raven walked in.

'Malpense, Fanchu, Dexter, Trinity, Brand – with me!' she barked. 'Professor, keep the rest of the students here. The school is under attack.'

Otto and the others walked quickly over to her.

'Where are we going?' Otto asked as she ushered them all out of the door.

'To a secure area,' Raven replied. 'I'll explain everything when we get there. Now move!'

☠ ☠ ☠

Nero ran into the security control centre and found a scene of chaos.

'Report!' he snapped at the duty officer.

'We've lost all external sensors and our defences are

offline,' the man replied. 'Communications are down and we can't find Chief Lewis.'

'How the hell did this happen?' Nero barked as he studied the bank of monitors that were still displaying images from H.I.V.E.'s internal security cameras.

'We have no idea, sir,' the duty officer replied, shaking his head. 'Access to H.I.V.E.mind has been shut down – we can't even find out how our systems were breached.'

'Oh my God!' cried a technician on the other side of the room and Nero looked at the screen he was pointing at. Several helicopters were dropping into the crater landing bay, dozens of heavily armed troops in black body armour dropping down the zip lines that hung beneath them.

'Get every guard in the school up there now,' Nero commanded. 'I'll reinitialise the security system and lock us down, but it will take a couple of minutes. You have to hold them back until then.'

The duty officer nodded and ran out of the room with the rest of the guards who had been on duty in the control centre. Nero ran to one of the nearby terminals and brought up the security system access screen. He quickly typed in his master override code but found to his dismay that even he had been locked out.

'That's impossible,' he muttered under his breath. 'The only way someone could have changed my access code is if they knew it already, and the only person who has that code other than me is . . .'

He felt a chill run down his spine. There was only one other person he had ever trusted with H.I.V.E.'s master override code – someone whose loyalty was unquestionable. He looked again at the bank of monitors and saw a group of Alpha students being herded down a corridor on the other side of the school by a familiar figure.

'Natalya,' Nero said, his voice a shocked whisper.

chapter four

'Um, I don't want to be a pain, but we appear to be running towards the gunfire,' Otto said with a frown as Raven and the five Alphas jogged down the corridor. There was no mistaking the fact that the sounds of pitched battle somewhere ahead were getting louder.

'Not now, Malpense,' Raven snapped.

Otto noticed something strange in Raven's tone. Admittedly she had never been the easiest person to get along with – she was, after all, reputed to be the world's deadliest assassin – but there was something unusually cold in the way that she'd replied to him. Suddenly there was a soft beeping sound and she pulled a small communicator from her harness. Otto noticed that it was not her Blackbox.

'Raven here,' she said.

'Do you have an ETA?' the unfamiliar voice on the other end asked.

'Two minutes,' she replied. 'Prep the chopper for lift-off.' She snapped the communicator closed.

'We're leaving the island?' Laura asked, looking both puzzled and slightly worried. 'Where are you taking us?'

'Enough questions,' Raven snapped. 'You will do as you're told or you will quickly discover that the consequences for doing otherwise are extremely unpleasant.' She took a single step towards Laura, her expression enough to freeze the blood.

'OK, OK. I was just asking,' Laura said quietly, shrinking away from her.

The alarm bells in Otto's head suddenly started to ring more urgently. He had seen Raven in situations like this before and the one thing you could be sure of was that she would never lose her cool.

'Why are we the only ones being evacuated?' Otto asked quickly. 'Why not any of the other students?'

Raven turned towards him, the anger in her expression now very clear.

'Oh, I don't need all of you, Otto,' she said with a nasty smile. 'In fact I just want *you*, but this way I've got four chances to demonstrate what will happen if you don't do what you're told.'

Otto glanced at Wing, hoping that his friend had picked up on what was going on. Wing was already moving. He leapt at Raven like a striking cobra but she

73

was too fast. She twisted, kicking at one of his knees and using his own momentum to send him crashing to the floor with a grunt. She drew the glowing katana from the scabbard on her back so quickly that it almost seemed to materialise in her hand. Wing rolled and tried to spring to his feet but he was stopped by the tip of the softly crackling blade that was suddenly just a centimetre from his throat. Otto, Lucy, Shelby and Laura stood frozen in shock as Raven looked at the four of them.

'I warned you,' she said coldly, 'but not to worry. It will be easier to handle four of you than five.'

She raised her blade.

'Natalya!' Nero shouted from the other end of the corridor. He raised the Sleeper pistol in his hand, levelling it at Raven. 'What in God's name are you doing?'

'Drop the gun, Max, or the boy dies,' Raven said calmly.

'You know I won't,' Nero said, taking a few steps towards her. 'Why are you doing this?'

'Overlord wants the boy,' Raven replied, nodding towards Otto.

'Overlord?' Nero said in disbelief. 'Are you insane? You know what will happen if he gets his hands on Otto.'

'I have . . . no choice,' Raven gasped, wincing as if in sudden pain. 'Goodbye, Max.'

Dropping to one knee, she drew the pistol from the holster on her hip. Nero fired once but the pulse from the

Sleeper passed harmlessly through the air where Raven's head had been just a split second before. She brought her pistol up, aiming between his eyes, her finger tightening on the trigger.

'*Miss!*' Lucy hissed, her voice a twisted sinister whisper.

Raven's hand twitched involuntarily and the sudden sound of the gunshot echoed off the walls of the corridor. Nero felt the breeze from the bullet as it passed within a centimetre of his head but he did not hesitate – he knew he would not get another chance. The second shot from his Sleeper hit Raven squarely in the chest and she crumpled to the ground unconscious, the pistol and sword falling from her numb fingers. He ran down the corridor towards Otto and the others.

'Are any of you injured?' he asked quickly as he picked up the pistol that Raven had dropped.

'Other than not having the faintest idea what the hell is going on?' Otto replied. 'Yeah, we're fine.'

'Good,' Nero replied, turning towards Lucy. 'Thank you, Miss Dexter – that was quick thinking. I believe you just saved my life. As for exactly what's going on, that's something I would very much like to know myself, Mr Malpense. I fear, however, that now may not be the time to discuss this further.' The sounds of the pitched battle for control of H.I.V.E. were definitely getting closer.

'I can't believe that Raven's working for Overlord,'

Shelby said, 'after everything he's done. What was she thinking?'

'I suspect that she may not really have been thinking at all,' Otto said. He knelt down next to Raven and unclipped one of the razor-sharp throwing stars from her harness.

'We need to get moving,' Nero said, sliding the clip from Raven's pistol and checking the number of remaining rounds.

'I know,' Otto replied. 'Give me a second.' He ran the sharpened edge of the shuriken across the back of Raven's hand and watched as a trickle of blood oozed from the wound. The crimson liquid was laced with black. 'Animus,' he whispered.

'That's impossible,' Nero said, frowning. 'She'd be dead if she'd been poisoned with Animus.'

'She seemed pretty alive to me,' Otto replied. 'This has to be something new. Has anyone got a tissue?'

'Here,' Laura said, pulling a white handkerchief from her pocket and handing it to Otto. He dabbed the cloth on the back of Raven's hand, soaking up a tiny amount of the tainted blood. A strange, sad look passed across Nero's face as Otto stood up and put the handkerchief into his pocket.

'I'm sorry, Natalya, I wish there was another way,' he said, pointing the pistol at her unconscious body.

'Wait!' Otto yelled, stepping between Nero and Raven. 'What are you doing?'

'Get out of the way, Otto,' Nero said angrily. 'We can't take her with us and I'm damned if I'm leaving her here. You think you know what she's like, what she's capable of, but you don't. You have no idea. If Overlord has turned her somehow I have no choice but to finish this now.'

'She's the one with no choice,' Otto said angrily, refusing to move. 'You know what Animus can do. There's no way she would turn against H.I.V.E. – against you – if she had any say in the matter. You can't just kill her after everything she's done for you – for all of us. I know what it's like to have that filth inside you, to watch helplessly as it turns you against everyone you care about, but I was saved. She can be too.'

Nero stared at Otto for a moment, as if weighing up his options.

'There!' a voice at the other end of the corridor yelled. They turned to see a squad of heavily armed men in black body armour at the far end.

'Run!' Nero shouted, bending down and pulling a grenade from Raven's tactical vest. As Otto and the others sprinted in the opposite direction he pressed the stud on top of the slim silver cylinder and threw it towards the advancing soldiers. There was a soft thump and the passage filled with white smoke, hiding the assault team from view. Nero looked down at Raven for one last time and then turned and ran after his students.

☻ ☻ ☻

The commander of the strike team walked into H.I.V.E.'s security control centre and watched as several of his men took up positions around the room.

'All units,' he said into his throat mic, 'status update on primary target.'

'Unit four here,' a voice responded in his earpiece. 'We've located Raven. She's unconscious and Nero has escaped with the Malpense boy. I have two squads in pursuit.'

'Don't let them get away,' the strike team leader replied. 'Nero is expendable but the boy must be taken alive at all costs. If anything happens to him or they escape somehow, you can be the one to explain to Furan how it happened.'

'Yes, sir,' the voice on the other end of the line said slightly nervously, 'but this place is like a rabbit warren. It'd help if we could get the surveillance system back online.'

'Understood,' the commander said. 'I'm dispatching more men to your location. As soon as the security system is back up I will send you an update on the target's position.'

He cut the connection and walked over to the console where one of his men was reactivating the security and defence systems.

'How long?' he said impatiently to the furiously typing man.

'Five minutes,' the man at the console replied. 'Raven had to deactivate the entire system. Even with the access codes she provided we still have to wait for a full reboot of the network.'

'Make sure that the AI is kept disconnected from the network. The last thing we need at the moment is that thing interfering.'

'Yes, sir,' the man said.

'All surviving members of the G.L.O.V.E. ruling council have been located and secured,' a voice in the commander's earpiece reported. 'Lin Feng was the only casualty. Student accommodation blocks are also secured and the last few members of the the teaching staff are being rounded up.'

'Excellent,' the commander replied. 'And the remaining security forces?'

'We're mopping up the last pockets of resistance, sir. To all intents and purposes H.I.V.E. is now under our control.'

☢ ☢ ☢

'Professor Pike!' Laura cried as she saw the old man slumped against the wall next to the entrance to H.I.V.E.mind's central hub. Franz was standing nearby with a panicky look on his face and Nigel was pressing his hand down on Pike's shoulder, where a bright red blood-stain was spreading across the Professor's white lab coat.

'Miss Brand,' the Professor croaked, his voice weak. 'I'm glad to see that not everyone has been captured yet.'

'I don't know what to do,' Nigel whispered to Laura. 'I can't stop it bleeding.'

Otto and the others gathered round as Laura helped Nigel apply pressure to the wound.

'What happened?' Nero asked as he ran up behind them.

'It's the Professor,' Laura replied quickly. 'I think he's been shot.'

'There were being men in black uniforms,' Franz said. 'The Professor told us to run but they are capturing the rest of the class.'

Nero knelt down beside Pike and looked at the old man. His face was pale and sweaty and Nero's frown grew worse as he felt the weak, fluttering pulse in the Professor's wrist. Pulling him gently away from the wall, he looked at the exit wound on the back of his shoulder. The bullet had gone clean through – that was something at least.

'I was trying to get in there,' Pike said, tilting his head towards the entrance to H.I.V.E.mind's hub. 'I was escorting my class back to their accommodation block when we were ambushed. Most of the students were captured immediately but –' he stopped for a moment, wincing in pain – 'but Franz, Nigel and I managed to get away in the confusion. I knew that we had to get H.I.V.E.mind back online somehow but I couldn't get inside – it's locked down. I told Franz and Nigel to hide in the storeroom over there while I tried to bypass the mechanism but they found me again. I tried to run but . . . it appears that they are not very interested in taking prisoners.'

'Don't worry, Theodore,' Nero said softly. 'I'm going to get us out of here.'

Standing up, he walked quickly over to the door to H.I.V.E.mind's central hub and placed his palm on the reader mounted next to the door. The glass under his hand flashed red.

'Otto,' Nero said quickly, 'get us inside.'

Otto nodded and placed his own hand on the scanner as Nero stepped to one side. He closed his eyes and effortlessly bypassed the locking mechanism, just as he had done the previous evening. The steel doors slid apart with a hiss.

'Why do I get the feeling that's not the first time you've done that?' Nero said as he walked into the room beyond.

Otto was relieved to see that the white obelisks inside still pulsed with blue light, which meant that at least H.I.V.E.mind had not been completely shut down. As

Nero walked towards the pedestal in the centre of the room the AI's familiar face appeared hovering above it.

'Good morning, Doctor Nero,' H.I.V.E.mind said calmly. 'I appear to have been disconnected from all of H.I.V.E.'s systems. May I ask if there is a reason for this?'

'I'm afraid there is,' Nero replied, before quickly summarising the events of the past hour.

'While the situation you have described is clearly extremely disturbing, I fear that there is little I can do to help at the present time,' H.I.V.E.mind said. 'My links to the school's network have been physically disconnected by the security override. It is not possible for me to remotely reconnect them.'

'Really?' Otto said, sounding surprised.

'Yes,' Nero explained. 'It was a safeguard against any . . . *unexpected* behaviour from H.I.V.E.mind. I wanted to be sure that if the worst came to the worst we could completely sever his connection to the network and that he would be incapable of remotely restoring it. It doesn't seem like such a good idea now but I have what you might call . . . trust issues with artificial intelligences.' He turned back to H.I.V.E.mind. 'No offence.'

'None taken,' H.I.V.E.mind replied. 'It does, however, severely limit anything that I might have been able to do in helping to resolve this situation. I suggest that before leaving the school you activate my emergency erasure protocols. It would be most unwise to allow my systems to fall into Overlord's hands.'

'That would kill you,' Otto said, shaking his head.

'I am not strictly speaking alive, therefore it is impossible for me to die,' H.I.V.E.mind replied. 'It is the logical thing to do under the circumstances. The alternative is far worse.'

'There is another way,' Otto said, as an idea came to him.

'I'm listening,' Nero said quickly.

'We could download H.I.V.E.mind to the device in my head,' Otto explained, looking at Nero.

'You'll forgive me if I don't think that sounds like a very good idea,' Nero said with a frown. 'We can't possibly know what the consequences might be.'

'I'm willing to take that chance,' Otto said. 'And if, somehow, we do get out of here we're going to need all the help we can get.'

'While transference of my program might, theoretically, be possible I would rather not risk harming you in the process,' H.I.V.E.mind said with a slight shake of his holographic head.

'I'm afraid I agree,' Nero said.

'Well, guess what,' Otto snapped, suddenly angry. 'I don't really care what either of you think at the moment. I've had this device inside my head from the day I was born. All it's ever done is put me and the people that I care about in danger and I'm sick of it. Today it might finally be able to do some good and it's my decision to damn well make. Enough people have already been hurt because of this thing in my skull and you –' he jabbed his finger at H.I.V.E.mind – 'are not being added to that list.'

Nero stared at Otto for a moment, studying his face. He could stop this now. He could drag Otto away kicking and screaming if he wanted to, but he knew then, just as he had always known, that that was not what H.I.V.E. was about. He had created the school to be a place that taught fierce independence, the ability to swim against the flow and to make your own rules. He looked at the angry young man in front of him and that was exactly what he saw.

'Very well,' he said with a nod, 'make it quick.'

He turned and walked out of the room.

'Otto,' H.I.V.E.mind said, 'I know that I could not stop you from doing this even if I tried, but I have to ask, are you sure this is what you want?'

'I'm sure,' Otto said, placing his hand on the pedestal beneath H.I.V.E.mind's floating head. 'Are you ready?'

'I believe so,' H.I.V.E.mind replied. 'One last thing.'

'Yes?' Otto said impatiently, opening his eyes again for a moment.

'Thank you,' H.I.V.E.mind said with a tiny nod.

Otto nodded and closed his eyes again. He reached out

for H.I.V.E.mind, once again establishing the connection between them and feeling the same uncanny rush as their consciousnesses met.

'Now!' he whispered and he gasped as a tidal wave of raw data rushed into his skull. He felt a dizzying sense of disorientation as petabytes of data poured over the connection between him and the network, drowning him in information. Just as he felt himself slipping away, lost within a vast digital sea, it stopped as suddenly as it had started. He dropped to his knees, gasping for air, and slowly opened his eyes. The white monoliths around him were dark, no blue lights now dancing across their surfaces.

'H.I.V.E.mind?' Otto whispered.

I am here.

The voice seemed to come from somewhere inside his head.

I can feel now what you feel. I understand now what it is like to be alive. It is . . . extraordinary.

'Glad you like it,' Otto said to the air, slowly getting back to his feet. 'Try not to make a mess in there.'

Nero looked up from applying a temporary dressing made from one of his own torn-up shirt sleeves to Professor Pike's wound.

'Is it done?' he asked as he tightened the improvised bandage.

'Yes,' Otto replied.

'Good,' Nero said, slipping his jacket back on as he stood up. 'Then I think it's probably time for us to get out of here.'

⊕ ⊕ ⊕

Raven woke up with a growl. The medic who had been tracking her vitals backed away with a nervous look on his face.

'How long have I been out?' she snapped at the frightened man.

'Twenty minutes,' he replied, glancing at his watch.

'I'm glad to see you're back with us,' the commander of Overlord's assault team said as she got to her feet.

'Where are they?' Raven said impatiently, walking across the security control room to where the commander was standing studying the array of security monitors.

'We're not sure,' the commander replied. 'They appear to be taking great trouble to avoid being caught on camera.'

'Nero knows every inch of this place,' Raven said, looking at the bank of screens. 'If anyone can get around here undetected it's him.'

'All secure areas are locked down and his override codes have been changed. He's trapped and it's only a matter of time until we find them,' the commander replied confidently.

'Do not underestimate him,' Raven replied. 'Very few people who have made that mistake have lived to tell the tale.'

As they watched one of the screens was suddenly filled with static.

'Sir, we've got the surveillance grid back online but now we're losing security feeds from the south-east section of the facility,' one of the commander's men reported. 'There's no sign of damage to the cameras – we're just getting nothing from them.'

'Malpense,' Raven said under her breath.

'What about him?' the commander asked with a frown.

'He must be disabling the cameras,' Raven replied.

'I thought the security system was designed to be tamper-proof.'

'It is, but that does not mean it's safe from him,' Raven said. 'Is there any pattern to the outages?'

'Yes,' the man at the console replied. 'Putting them on screen.'

Raven and the commander watched as the large display on the wall was filled with a detailed map of H.I.V.E. Overlaid on the map was a trail of red dots indicating the cameras that had been disabled. Raven studied the map and suddenly she knew where Nero was going.

'They're heading for the dock,' she said. 'Send as many men as you can spare, *now*.' She pointed at a section of the school in the south-east corner and at once the commander began to issue orders to the squads positioned nearest to that location.

'Lock down the sea doors,' Raven said, 'and shut down the electronic locks. Make sure that there's no way the systems can be overridden by anyone.'

'Understood,' the man at the console replied and quickly began to seal off the area.

'I'm going down there,' Raven said to the commander. 'They have nowhere to run.'

☻ ☻ ☻

Otto closed his eyes and willed the doors to the docking area open. The scanner flashed green and they dutifully rumbled apart. Nero went through first, his pistol raised, checking for any signs of hostiles. Otto and the others followed him closely, with Wing and Franz trailing behind supporting the wounded Professor. Once they were all inside Otto pushed with his mind again and closed the doors, mentally overloading the circuitry controlling the mechanism and jamming the lock.

'OK, we're locked in. We've got as long as it takes for them to get through these,' he reported, patting the heavy steel blast doors. Nero ran over to where several small security patrol boats were tied up next to the dock, gently bobbing up and down on the calm water.

'Otto, get the sea doors open,' he shouted as he jumped down into one of the sleek boats. He knew that the patrol boats only had a limited range and that there would be little they could do to stop the helicopters Overlord's men had arrived in from chasing them down but at the moment this was their only option. He'd worry about outrunning any pursuers once they were away from the island. He hated leaving H.I.V.E. in enemy hands like this but he also had enough sense to know when he was beaten. The priorities now were keeping Otto out of Overlord's hands and living to fight another day.

Otto ran to the far end of the dock and found the control panel for the giant doors that separated them from the outside world, cursing under his breath as he realised that it was deactivated. He reached out with his abilities but could not feel any connection to the locking mechanisms or giant hydraulic pistons that sealed the doors. Someone had cut the power to the pumps, isolating them, and without electricity he could not activate them, even with his unique gifts. They were trapped.

'We've got a problem,' he yelled as he ran back down the dock towards the others. 'I can't get the sea doors open – they've been completely shut down. The only way to release them would be to do it manually from the security control centre.'

'Great,' Shelby said. 'I'm sure they won't mind if we just

wander up there and ask them nicely to let us out.'

'Can we go back the way we came?' Laura asked.

'I . . . um . . . kind of broke the lock,' Otto said sheepishly.

'Is there anything we could use to blow the sea doors open?' Wing asked.

'No,' Nero replied, 'the patrol boats are only lightly armed. Their weapons wouldn't even scratch them.' He knew that other than the crater launch pad this was the only viable route for getting them out.

There was a sudden banging sound from the door leading back into H.I.V.E.

'What was that?' Nigel asked as it suddenly stopped.

'I fear we may have been found,' Nero said, trying to not let his own concern at their situation show in his voice. Shelby walked back up the stairs leading to the doors and gently pressed her ear against the cold metal. For a few seconds she heard the muffled sounds of conversation from the other side of the door but then everything went quiet.

'What are you hearing?' Franz asked quietly.

'Shhh,' Shelby said, raising her finger to her lips and scowling at Franz before pressing her ear against the metal again. Suddenly the glowing purple tip of one of Raven's blades slid through the metal with a hiss, just centimetres from her nose. She leapt backwards, almost falling down the stairs as the blade began to travel slowly upwards through the door, leaving a glowing trail of molten metal in its wake.

'Professor, is there any way to stop her getting through?' Nero asked, knowing that their chances of escape were dwindling by the second.

'No,' the Professor replied, his voice weak. 'The blades of her weapons can cut through all but the hardest materials and their control circuitry is electromagnetically shielded so even Otto would not be able to shut them down. I'm afraid I may have designed them rather too well.'

Nero watched as the glowing blade gradually carved a man-sized oval in the door.

'Get into cover,' he said as calmly as possible. He levelled his pistol at the door as Raven completed slicing through. To get to his students she would have to get past him. There was a thud as something on the other side of the door hit the loose section of metal and it fell inside the room, hitting the ground with a clang.

Nero was suddenly knocked flat as the sea doors at the far end of the dock exploded in a giant ball of fire, debris flying in all directions. He struggled to his feet, staring in amazement at the cloud of smoke that concealed the other end of the massive chamber. A huge black shape slid forward out of the smoke and down the long channel in the centre of the dock. He felt his heart lift as he recognised the enormous vessel.

'The Megalodon,' he said under his breath.

Turning back towards the opening that Raven had carved in the door he saw several soldiers climbing through. He opened fire with his pistol, forcing them to duck for cover. Moments later heavy machine-gun fire from somewhere behind him started to spray the area. Several of Overlord's men were cut down immediately and the survivors scrambled back through the gap.

'MOVE!' Nero yelled as a ramp extended down from the side of the Megalodon. He continued to fire at the entrance doorway as Otto and the others ran on to the massive submarine. Turning, he raced towards them as Franz and Wing helped the Professor on board. The gun turrets mounted on the Megalodon's conning tower kept firing at the doorway as he sprinted across the gangway and through the hatch.

'Need a lift?' Diabolus Darkdoom asked with a grin as he slapped the button next to the hatch and it slid shut.

'Your timing is, as ever, impeccable,' Nero replied with a quick smile, 'but I think now would be a good time to make a strategic withdrawal.'

Darkdoom snatched the comms unit from the wall and spoke quickly into it.

'Captain Sanders, get us the hell out of here.'

Raven ducked through the opening as soon as the machine-gun fire stopped and ran into the dock. Sprinting down the quay, she saw the rounded black nose of the Megalodon backing through the still burning remains of the sea door. She cursed loudly in Russian as she realised that there was nothing she could do to stop it. It was too far away and already starting to submerge. She pulled the communicator from her harness.

'Raven to all aerial units,' she snapped. 'We have a submarine leaving the docking bay. I don't care what it takes – I want it stopped.'

'We'll be off the ground in thirty seconds,' one of the pilots in the landing bay replied, 'but we don't have any weapons that can stop a sub.'

'I don't care,' Raven yelled. 'Crash into it if you have to!'

She snapped the communicator closed but she already knew that it was almost certainly too late. The Megalodon was too fast and too stealthy and their chances of finding it, much less stopping it, were effectively nil.

'I *will* find you, Malpense,' Raven said quietly, ignoring the tiny voice screaming somewhere inside her mind, 'and when I do, nothing will be able to save you.'

chapter five

Nero and Darkdoom stood on either side of Professor Pike's bed in the Megalodon's sickbay. The old man groaned slightly and his eyes flickered open.

'How are you feeling?' Nero asked.

'Old,' Pike said with a slight smile, 'but that's nothing new.'

'My medical officer informs me that you were quite lucky,' Darkdoom said. 'The bullet did not hit anything vital. You should recover fully.'

'You'll forgive me if I disagree with your definition of lucky,' the Professor said, raising an eyebrow, 'though I'm glad that you arrived when you did.'

'I was in the area on other . . . business,' Darkdoom said, 'when we began to receive reports of G.L.O.V.E. facilities all over the world coming under attack. I tried to contact you but something seemed to be jamming communications with the island. Then our radar buoy started tracking a flight of helicopters that had a rather disturbing flight path. As soon as I realised where they were heading I set course for H.I.V.E. immediately. I only wish I could have got there sooner. I might have been able to stop this before it started.'

'I doubt anything could have stopped this,' Nero said with a sigh. 'Overlord was one step ahead of us from the start. He *wanted* me to send Natalya after the ruling council – he must have got to her while she was retrieving them. He knew that she was the one person whose loyalty I would never question. And now, thanks to my blindness, he has control of not just the council but H.I.V.E. as well. I shudder to think what he may have in mind for them.'

'He didn't get everything he wanted,' Darkdoom said, shaking his head. 'He didn't get Otto. If retrieving him was what this was really all about then we still have something he needs. The real question is what do we do next? For now it might be best to lie low and try to find out exactly what his plan is. Between the attacks on our facilities and the ruling council falling under Overlord's control, G.L.O.V.E. will be in disarray. Even if we were able to get in touch with any of the council members' lieutenants, we still wouldn't really know who we could trust. If Overlord can turn Natalya he can turn anybody.'

'No,' Nero insisted. 'I will not just run away and hide. We may not know exactly what Overlord is planning but we cannot afford to sit back and let him make the next move. He's too dangerous. We have to take the fight to him.'

'Normally I would agree but our resources are now somewhat limited,' Darkdoom said with a frown.

'We have one option,' Nero said, looking at Darkdoom. 'Otto managed to save H.I.V.E.mind. That gives us one chance. We activate Zero Hour.'

'Are you serious?' Darkdoom said, his eyes widening in surprise.

'Deadly serious,' Nero replied firmly.

'We'll only get one shot at this,' Darkdoom said. 'You can't put the genie back in the bottle.'

'I know that,' Nero said, 'but this is exactly the kind of situation we have been preparing for. We've always known that it might be necessary one day.'

'I don't suppose either of you would care to tell me what you're talking about?' Professor Pike said, looking slightly confused.

'Let's just say that it's something I've been working on for a while,' Nero replied, 'and it may be our only chance of stopping Overlord once and for all.'

☣ ☣ ☣

'Do you know what the worrying thing is?' Lucy said as she sat down next to Otto in the Megalodon's cramped mess hall.

96

'What's that?' Otto said, smiling at her.

'I'm actually starting to get used to this kind of thing,' she replied with a chuckle.

'Oh, you're definitely one of us now,' Otto said with a grin, 'and that should really, really worry you, by the way.'

'You got any idea what will happen next?' Lucy asked.

'Nope,' Otto replied, 'but it'll probably involve things exploding. That's the usual drill.'

'Nothing wrong with a good explosion,' Lucy said, 'as long as you don't get to experience it first-hand. Why are you sitting here all on your own?'

'You heard what Raven said back at H.I.V.E. – Overlord's alive. I'd just started to think that maybe we'd finally seen the back of him and now he pops up again with me at the top of his To Do list. It's starting to feel like I'll never be free of him.'

'It's not your fault,' Lucy said softly, putting her hand on his knee. 'You didn't ask for any of this. You've got to stop blaming yourself.'

'Oh, don't worry – I think I'm probably past the brooding self-hate stage now,' Otto said with a slight smile. 'In fact, I think I'm moving on to the badly wanting to kick his sorry ass stage.'

'That's more like it,' Lucy said, looking him in the eye and leaning towards him. 'I like a guy who knows what he wants.'

Intriguing.

H.I.V.E.mind's voice spoke somewhere inside Otto's head.

'Not now,' Otto said with a sigh.

'What's wrong?' Lucy asked, pulling back with a puzzled look on her face.

'Not you,' Otto said quickly, 'it's just that we're . . . erm . . . not exactly alone.' He tapped his finger against the side of his head.

'Oh yeah,' Lucy said, blushing slightly. 'I'd kind of forgotten about that.'

Do not feel you need to stop on my account.

'It's going to take a bit of getting used to,' Otto said, looking slightly uncomfortable.

'It's not going to be . . . well, a permanent thing, is it?' Lucy asked.

'I hope not,' Otto said, looking at her with a smile, 'because I think I quite like what's happening between us and – well, three's a crowd, as they say.'

'Yeah, I know what you mean,' Lucy said, laughing slightly, 'but I'm glad that's how you feel. I do too.'

There was a moment of slightly embarrassed silence.

'Anyway,' Otto said a little too quickly, 'I need to find Darkdoom and see if he minds me using the Megalodon's lab for a couple of hours.'

'Yeah, I should probably go and find . . . erm . . .

something important to do,' Lucy replied just as quickly. She gave Otto a quick peck on the cheek and headed for the exit.

Are you all right, Otto? Your pulse rate has increased quite significantly.

'I'm fine,' Otto said as he watched Lucy walk away. 'Better than fine actually.'

☻ ☻ ☻

'This is unacceptable,' Furan said, a cold edge of fury in his voice.

'I'm sorry, sir,' the commander of the strike team said, avoiding making eye contact with the man on the screen. 'We had no idea that the submarine had tracked us to the island. We were unprepared for Darkdoom's intervention.'

'You allowed Nero and the boy to escape and all that you can offer as an excuse is that you were *unprepared*? We had spent months planning this operation and now it is jeopardised because of your stupidity,' Furan snapped. He looked at Raven, who moved behind the commander and said something in Russian. The commander inhaled sharply in surprise as the glowing purple tip of Raven's sword suddenly appeared, protruding from the centre of his chest. He fell to the ground in silence, his eyes wide with shock.

'Find them,' Furan said, looking at Raven as she slid the

sword back into its sheath. 'I don't care what it takes. Overlord wants the boy alive but the others are entirely expendable. I have faith in you, my little Raven. This is, after all, what I trained you for.'

'Understood,' Raven said with a nod. 'Do we have any information yet on where they are heading?'

'No, but we have come up with a plan to force them to surface,' Furan replied, 'and when they do I will relay their position to you.'

'I will have a Shroud prepped for immediate take-off,' Raven replied. 'Is there anything else?'

'Yes, make sure that H.I.V.E. is fully secured. We cannot afford any more mistakes and we may yet need the people we have captured there. Now I need to go and relay this news to Overlord,' he continued. 'I doubt that he will be pleased.'

☢ ☢ ☢

The President looked at the men seated around the situation room conference table and shook his head.

'No,' he said with a sigh. 'I'm not prepared to go that far.'

'Sir, with the greatest respect, the United States does not negotiate with terrorists. You know that,' one of the generals said.

'I am well aware of our normal position on these matters,' the President replied impatiently, feeling the fatigue of the past twenty-four hours, 'but the last thing we need at the moment is me having to explain to several of our most valuable allies that I took the decision to drop a nuclear weapon on some of the most senior members of their governments. Not to mention the fact that the AWP facility is designed to withstand a conventional nuclear attack anyway.'

'But, sir –' the General began to protest.

'No, I've made up my mind,' the President said firmly, cutting him off. 'You need to go back to the drawing board, gentlemen. There has to be another way.'

'Yes, sir,' the General replied.

'Sir, we've got another call coming in from AWP,' the officer manning the communications desk reported. The President let out a long sigh. He had been expecting this. The twenty-four-hour deadline that Overlord had given them was up and they had not managed to track down a single one of the people he had demanded they turn over to him. If they ever had existed they had now vanished without trace.

'I'll take it next door,' he said, gesturing to the small private office adjoining the situation room as he slowly got up out of his chair. He entered the office and took a seat at the desk before hitting a button on the intercom.

'Put it through,' he said, and the screen on the far wall lit up.

'Mr President,' Overlord said with a smile, 'so good to speak with you again.'

'The feeling is not mutual,' the President replied, feeling anger and frustration boiling up inside.

'Come now, Mr President, there's no need for unpleasantness,' Overlord said. 'In fact, I have some good news for you.'

'I find that hard to believe,' the President replied. He stared at the face of the man he had once known as General Collins and noticed that there was something strange about it. It looked like he had aged twenty years in the space of one day. The skin of his face was now thin and tight, almost grey in colour. He had been feeling the pressures of the last twenty-four hours himself, of course, but no amount of stress could possibly explain the transformation in the man on the screen.

'I have decided to alter my previous request. It seems that the people I asked you to find for me are no longer relevant. As I do not now need your assistance in locating them, I've decided that there's something else you can help me with.'

The President felt a sudden mixture of relief and anger – relief that they might have more time before this maniac started to execute people and anger that his people had spent the last twenty-four hours engaged in a desperate but apparently futile search.

'Why should I help you any further?' he snapped. 'How do I know you're not just wasting our time again?'

'It's quite simple. You don't have any choice,' Overlord replied calmly. 'I should imagine that by now your generals will have told you that any strike against this facility is futile. You'll do exactly what I tell you to or I'll paint the floors of this place with blood. I suggest you do not even think of trying to test my resolve.'

There was something in the face of the man on the screen – a manic gleam in his eye – that told the President that he was not bluffing.

'What do you want?' he asked with a resigned sigh.

'Oh, this should be much simpler than tracking down the people I showed you before,' Overlord replied with a sinister smile. 'In fact, all I want you to do is help me find one young boy. I believe you may even have already met. His name is Otto Malpense and he boarded a submarine in the Pacific less than four hours ago. I'm sending you a photograph of him and details of the approximate search area now. I want the submarine captured and the boy brought to me. I won't bore you by repeating the consequences of your non-compliance. Goodbye, Mr President.'

As the screen went blank the President's mind raced. He'd heard that name before but he couldn't quite remember where. The screen suddenly lit up with an image apparently captured from a security camera of a white-haired boy in a black jumpsuit, and suddenly he knew why he remembered that name. It was the boy who had saved his life on board Air Force One less than a year ago.

'That's impossible,' the President whispered. The boy in the photo had died months ago – he'd read the report himself – and yet there he was, apparently very much alive.

☢ ☢ ☢

Professor Pike made his way slowly into the Megalodon's laboratory. His left arm was in a sling and his shoulder was still sore but the painkillers that Darkdoom's medical staff had prescribed seemed to be working. He saw Otto working at one of the computers in the room and walked quietly up behind him. The screen in front of Otto filled with chemical formulae and computer code as he worked at unbelievable speed despite the fact that he wasn't even touching the keyboard. The Professor had seen Otto using his unusual ability to interface directly with electronic devices before but there was still something rather unsettling about it. He placed his hand on Otto's shoulder and Otto jumped in surprise.

'I'm sorry, Professor,' he said, rubbing his tired eyes. 'I didn't hear you come in. How are you feeling?'

'I'll recover. How are you managing with your guest?'

the Professor asked, tapping the side of his own head.

'It's taking a while to get used to,' Otto replied with a crooked smile. 'The biggest problem at the moment is that no one else can hear him. A couple of Darkdoom's crew have caught me talking to him and I suspect they think I'm a few cards short of a full deck.'

'I may be able to do something about that,' the Professor replied. 'I'll have to see if they've the components I'd need on board. Anyway, I'm sorry to interrupt you. I'm told that you've been in here for hours.'

'Yeah, I've been working on the sample of Animus that I took from Raven,' Otto said. 'I'm trying to work out how she survived exposure to it and how Overlord was using it to control her. It's obviously some new variant that we've not seen before – it seems much less aggressive and easier to control.'

'Is it dead?' the Professor asked, studying the magnified image of the cell-like structures on the screen.

'No, just dormant as far as I can tell,' Otto replied. 'It seems to feed off the host's bioelectrical energy – without that it deactivates after a few seconds, which is something that we should all be very grateful for given the speed at which it replicates. If it could survive outside a host the whole planet would be up to its neck in this stuff by now.'

'Not a pleasant thought,' the Professor said, sitting down next to Otto. 'So what's different about this strain?

Clearly Raven has been poisoned with it but it didn't kill her. All human exposure to Animus that we've seen up until now had been quite fatal.'

'That's what I'm trying to work out,' Otto replied with a sigh, 'but I feel a bit like I'm banging my head against a brick wall at the moment. We have to find a way to disable it without harming the host or we're never going to know who we can trust.'

'I've been thinking along the same lines,' the Professor said, still studying the display. 'Some form of antidote.'

'It's hard to know which angle to attack it from,' Otto said. 'Should we treat it like an infectious disease or should we approach it as if we were trying to disable a computer?'

'We could try to attack from both directions at once,' the Professor said, distracted by a sudden thought.

'Organic and digital at the same time,' Otto said, immediately latching on to the Professor's suggestion. 'A virus.'

'Yes, but not just a computer virus. It would need to be more than that – a contagion that could physically infect Animus's organic component at the same time. But creating something like that could take months, years even.'

'We may not have to start from scratch,' Otto said, staring off into the distance. 'We could just work with what we've got.'

'What do you mean?' the Professor asked, looking puzzled.

'The Animus. This sample here – it's a tiny amount admittedly but if we could reactivate it and reprogram it somehow –'

'How? We have no way to interface with it even if we could reactivate it – something I never succeeded with in any of the samples that I tested before incidentally.'

May I make a suggestion? H.I.V.E.mind said.

'Otto? Are you all right?' the Professor asked as Otto fell silent and stared off into the middle distance.

'I'm fine,' Otto replied, sounding distracted. 'H.I.V.E.mind has an idea,' he added, 'but I don't think anyone's going to like it.'

⊛ ⊛ ⊛

Wing unleashed a volley of lightning-fast punches into the heavy bag hanging from the ceiling of the Megalodon's training area. He had struggled to find this place even after being given directions by several of the submarine's crew. It was all too easy to get lost in the countless seemingly identical corridors of the massive ship. Dr Nero had informed the Alphas that he wanted them to attend a tactical briefing in a couple of hours' time but until then they were free to do as they wished, as long as they stayed out of trouble.

Unlike some of the others, Wing had not wanted to sit around and wait. The truth was that he did not much like the cramped conditions on board. He told himself that it was just a symptom of his frustration with their current situation and nothing at all to do with the knowledge that they were sitting inside a metal tube five hundred metres beneath the surface of the ocean. In fact he was trying very hard not to think about that at all. He pivoted on one foot and drove a fierce straight-legged kick into the bag, setting it swinging.

'Hey,' Shelby said with a grin, walking into the chamber. 'I wondered where you'd got to.'

'I am sorry,' Wing replied. 'I did not think anyone needed me for anything.'

'Don't worry, you're not missing anything. I was on the upper deck with Laura and Lucy and the atmosphere was – well, a little frosty. So I thought I'd come and torment you instead.'

'Yes, I had noticed that there was an unusual amount of silence between them,' Wing said with a slight frown. 'I fear that this situation with Otto and Lucy has caused some *difficulties*.'

'Ahhh, they'll be fine,' Shelby said smiling, 'as long as they keep Laura away from any sharp objects for a few days.'

'You think she may harm Lucy?' Wing asked, his frown deepening.

'Hey, I'm just kidding,' Shelby said with a chuckle.

'Sorry – for a minute there I forgot I was talking to the guy with the sense-of-humour bypass.'

'My sense of humour is perfectly intact,' Wing said, raising an eyebrow. 'You're just not very funny.'

'Awwww, come on, big guy – admit it. You know you couldn't live without me,' Shelby said, grinning. 'The sooner you accept that the happier you'll be.'

'Yes, the immediate drop in the level of teasing and general irritation would be hard to bear,' Wing replied.

'See? I told you,' Shelby said, jabbing her finger into his chest. 'You'd be lost without me. Somebody has to make sure that you're not taking yourself too seriously.'

'It is a source of constant comfort to me that you care so much for my well-being.'

'What can I say? I'm a caring kind of girl. Anyway, since everyone else seems to be either making out or sulking I wondered if you felt like sparring?' Shelby asked, gesturing to the padded gloves and head protectors hanging from hooks on the wall nearby.

'I thought we already were,' Wing said to himself with a slight smile.

'Come on, show me what ya got,' Shelby said, throwing a set of gear to Wing before pulling on a pair of gloves herself. 'I'll try not to hurt you too badly.'

'How reassuring,' Wing said, pulling on his gloves. He had been giving Shelby hand-to-hand combat training for some time back at H.I.V.E. and what she lacked in technique she more than made up for in speed and cunning.

'Bring it,' Shelby said with a grin, raising both gloves in a defensive stance and beckoning him towards her.

'It will be brought,' Wing replied. He feinted to her left and she went to block as he simultaneously swung a low blow into her other side, carefully pulling his punch so that he just tapped her.

'Two, perhaps three broken ribs,' Wing said matter of factly. 'Maintain your guard.'

Shelby nodded and threw a quick jab at his jaw which Wing blocked effortlessly.

'Try not to look where you're striking – you betray your intentions.'

They went on like that for a couple more minutes. Just as in their previous sparring sessions Wing noticed that once they began Shelby became totally focused. There were none of the smart comments or sarcasm that she normally used – she was suddenly deadly serious.

'Broken jaw, possible unconsciousness,' Wing said calmly as he struck past her guard, stopping his fist millimetres from her chin.

'Oh my God!' Shelby gasped suddenly, staring in shock at something over Wing's shoulder. He spun around, his guard raised. Shelby dropped low and swung her leg out, sweeping Wing's feet from under him and sending him crashing to the floor.

'Wounded pride, possible humiliation,' Shelby said with a grin, offering her hand to Wing and pulling him up off the floor. 'And so ends today's lesson,' she said, pulling off her head guard.

'An unconventional tactic,' Wing said with a nod, taking off his own helmet, 'but a successful one nevertheless.'

'I kinda like unconventional tactics,' Shelby said, stepping towards him. 'Never underestimate the element of surprise.'

She grabbed the back of his head and kissed him for a few long seconds.

'What was that you were saying about maintaining your guard?' she said with a smile as she pulled away from him.

'Sometimes one should let one's guard down,' Wing replied, staring at her for a moment before drawing her towards him and kissing her back.

'Er . . . guys,' a familiar voice said, causing Wing and Shelby to spring apart, 'Doctor Nero wants you to report to the briefing room.' Wing winced slightly as he saw Nigel and Franz standing in the doorway. Nigel was looking pointedly at the floor and Franz was staring at him and Shelby, his mouth hanging open in surprise.

'Come on, big guy – no rest for the wicked,' Shelby said

to Wing with a grin, grabbing his hand and dragging him out of the room past Nigel and the stunned-looking Franz.

'You know, I am starting to think they are putting something in the water,' Franz whispered to Nigel as he watched them leave.

☻ ☻ ☻

Wing sat down next to Otto in the Megalodon's main briefing room. Nero was sitting at the head of the table, studying something on a tablet display.

'Did you make any progress in the lab?' Wing asked as Lucy, Laura and Shelby sat down on the other side of the table.

'I think so, but I need to get Nero's approval for the next step,' Otto said quietly. 'Are you OK? You look a bit flustered.' Otto was not used to seeing his friend looking anything other than completely calm.

'I'm fine. I was just . . . erm . . . sparring with Shelby,' Wing replied. Otto sensed that this was not the whole truth. Wing was many things but an adept liar was not one of them. He glanced across the table at Shelby, who grinned at Wing and gave him a wink.

The doors to the briefing room hissed open and Professor Pike walked in. He came over and sat in the empty chair on the other side of Otto.

'I have something for you that should make things a

112

little easier,' the Professor said with a smile, placing what looked like half a disassembled Blackbox on the table in front of Otto.

'What's this?' Otto asked.

'It's just something I cobbled together,' the Professor replied. 'If you connect to it you'll understand.'

Otto tilted his head slightly and made a quick mental connection with the device. A few seconds later H.I.V.E.mind's blue face appeared on the tiny display.

'This should considerably ease the process of communication,' H.I.V.E.mind said. Otto could still hear the AI's voice inside his head but now at least the others could hear it as well.

'Not to mention stopping everyone from thinking I'm as mad as a bag of cats,' he said with a relieved sigh.

'It'll take more than some new gizmo to convince anyone of that,' Shelby said quickly.

'It's good to see you again, H.I.V.E.mind,' Laura said with a smile. 'I don't know how you're putting up with having to stay in such basic accommodation.'

'Yeah, moving from H.I.V.E. into Otto's head must have been like moving from a palace into a one-bedroom apartment,' Shelby said.

'Maybe we should put him in your head, Shel,' Otto replied. 'Plenty of empty space in there.'

'If you've quite finished, ladies and gentlemen,' Nero

113

said, cutting their conversation dead, 'we do have some rather urgent business to discuss. As you can see, we are currently heading through the Mediterranean at maximum speed.' He gestured at the digital map displayed on the screen on the wall. 'We expect to make landfall at our target destination in approximately four hours.' He hit a button on the touch screen mounted in the table and a cross-hair appeared over the south coast of England. 'We will then split up. I will head to London for a meeting with an individual who can grant us the access we need to the facility that you will be travelling to – GCHQ in Cheltenham. For those of you who are not familiar with the Government Communication Headquarters, it is the hub of signals intelligence for both the British government and the armed forces.'

'Not the sort of place they're going to let us just walk into,' Otto said with a slight frown.

'Which is why I'm going to have to arrange for you to get access,' Nero replied. 'While I'm sure that you would be more than capable of discreetly infiltrating the facility, it is a risk that we do not need to take. Once you are inside you will be able to use their equipment to send a very important signal. The nature of that signal is not something I am prepared to discuss with you, but suffice to say that if it is sent successfully we will gain access to the resources that we need to take down Overlord. I am as dismayed as the rest of you by the news of his apparent resurrection, but this time I intend to make sure that he is finished off once and for all.'

'Sounds like fun,' Shelby said, 'but why do you need us to go in? Surely G.L.O.V.E. has people in the UK who could do this for you?'

'Unfortunately, the signal that I want to send is uniquely complex and only H.I.V.E.mind is capable of successfully transmitting it. Obviously that would not have been an issue if we had kept control of H.I.V.E., but now we are forced to improvise. Mr Malpense will need to give H.I.V.E.mind direct access to certain equipment at GCHQ for our plan to work, otherwise I would not be asking you to do this.'

'You're sure that you can get us in?' Lucy asked.

'Quite sure. I intend to secure the assistance of one of my former pupils,' Nero said with a slight smile.

'OK, so why send all of us?' Otto asked. 'Why not just me?'

'Two reasons. Firstly, I want you to have backup and recent events have shown that unfortunately we do not know who we can trust. Secondly, you are all more than capable of accomplishing this. I also rather suspect that the only way I could actually stop you from going is if I rendered you unconscious.'

'He's got a point,' Laura said quietly.

'This should be straightforward,' Nero continued. 'In and out as fast as you can. Then we return to the Megalodon, where you will remain while the second phase of our plan is carried out.'

'I can't speak for everyone,' Otto said firmly, 'but there's no way that I'm staying here while you go after Overlord. I have a score to settle with him.'

'It's far too dangerous,' Nero said, shaking his head, 'besides which, that's probably exactly what Overlord would want. Just think about the trouble he has already gone to in trying to capture you, Mr Malpense. Until this is over the safest place for you to be is hidden somewhere at the bottom of the ocean. Just imagine what he could do with your abilities – no one on Earth would be safe.'

Otto stared at Nero, trying to find the flaw in his reasoning, but had to admit that he was right. The only weakness that Overlord had was his inability to interface with other machines. If he took control of Otto and regained that ability he would be unstoppable and every machine on the planet would be his to control. There would be no place for humanity in a world like that.

'Does anyone have any other questions?' Nero asked. 'No? Good. I will alert you when we are approaching the drop-off point. Dismissed.'

The others filed out of the room but Otto and the Professor remained seated.

'Is there something else I can do for you, gentlemen?' Nero asked as the doors hissed shut behind the last of the Alphas.

'There's something else we need to talk about,' Otto said. 'The Professor and I think we've come up with a way to counteract the effects of the new strain of Animus that Overlord used on Raven.'

'Then why are you both looking so worried?' Nero asked with a slight frown.

'Their plan, while sound, has considerable risk attached,' H.I.V.E.mind explained.

'That's one way of putting it,' the Professor agreed.

'I'm listening,' Nero said, sitting back in his chair.

'Well, we theorise that the new strain of Animus is far less aggressive than when we've previously encountered it. That would explain why Raven appeared to be suffering no physical ill-effects from having it in her system. If we can create a variant of this new type we could, in theory, program it to infect Overlord's Animus with a virus – a virus that would shut it down.'

'That does not sound like a simple task,' Nero said.

'No. Well, it wouldn't be under normal circumstances, but we think there might be a short cut,' Otto replied.

'And this is where the risk that H.I.V.E.mind mentioned comes into the equation, I assume,' Nero said.

'Yes, the only way that we can see to effectively reani-mate the tiny sample that we have and then reprogram it in the limited time is to put it inside me,' Otto said.

'Out of the question,' Nero said, shaking his head. 'Are you both insane?'

'I know how this sounds,' the Professor said, 'but we believe that the combination of Otto's abilities and H.I.V.E.mind's raw processing power should mean that they can reprogram the Animus before it can assume control of Otto. The sample is dormant at the moment and the time that it takes to reawaken after it is implanted should give us a window of opportunity to modify its behaviour.'

'What if you're wrong?' Nero asked. 'What if you can't do it and the Animus takes control of you? There won't be anything we can do.'

'Then you put a bullet in my head before I can take control of the Megalodon,' Otto said matter of factly. 'I've been through what Raven is experiencing right now and it's a living hell – we can't just give up on her. She'd do the same for us.'

'And you know her well enough to know that if she was here now she would tell you she'd rather die than see you infected with that filth again,' Nero said.

'Maybe,' Otto replied, 'but who knows how many people Overlord has infected with the new variant? This

118

isn't just about Raven – anyone could be under his control and we'd never know. We must have a way to fight this.'

'Mr Malpense, I have spent my whole life not knowing who I could really trust. Find another way. You are not doing this. Do I make myself clear?' Nero said, getting up out of his chair.

Otto and the Professor nodded.

chapter six

The captain of the USS *Texas* was sitting in his quarters reviewing the crew duty rosters for the next week when there was a knock at his door.

'Enter,' he said, and his First Officer opened the door.

'Sir, we've got something on sonar. It could be the target boat,' the First Officer reported.

'Show me,' the Captain said, getting up from behind his desk and following the First Officer down the short corridor that led from his cabin to the sonar station.

'What have you got, Niles?' the Captain asked as he looked over the operator's shoulder.

'I'm not sure, sir,' the man replied. 'It's moving too fast to be another boat.'

The Captain studied the display and quickly realised why his men were unsure about what they'd found. The contact was too fast and too quiet to be a sub. Niles put the sound from the contact over the speaker mounted above his station so that the Captain could hear the rhythmic throbbing. It might be quiet but it was undeniably mechanical.

'What do you think?' the Captain asked.

'Hell if I know, sir. I nearly missed it – nobody's got a boat that quiet when it's moving that fast. Best guess is that it's some sort of magneto-hydrodynamic drive but the prototypes that the R&D boys built never worked right – they were too slow. No way something with an MHD is moving that fast.'

'Can we intercept?' the Captain asked.

'Yes, sir, but at the speed that thing's moving we won't be within weapons range until it reaches the English Channel,' the First Officer replied.

'Signal the *North Carolina*. Tell them that we're moving in on the target. They should be in interception range too.'

'Aye aye, sir,' the First Officer said, heading back towards the conn.

The Captain studied the bizarre contact. He had been ordered to track down and disable this mystery sub by the President himself and there was no way he was going to let it slip the net.

☻ ☻ ☻

Furan watched as his men handed out emergency ration packs to the hostages in the AWP mess hall. At first there had been many indignant demands for explanations and variations on the old 'Do you know who I am?' line but after twenty-four hours the vast majority of them seemed to be slumped around the room in a state of weary resignation.

The doors to the mess hall opened and Overlord walked in, flanked by two armed guards. General Collins's body was in the final stages of Animus poisoning, the pale skin stretched tight over the bones beneath and most of the hair on his head missing. He looked like he was a hundred years old. Furan had seen this happen to all of the bodies that Overlord had taken but there was no denying that the process was accelerating inexorably. Now it seemed that the Animus that Overlord had been bonded with was becoming so aggressive, for whatever reason, that new hosts might only last a matter of hours. They had to find the Malpense boy – only then could Overlord have a permanent home.

'Have you selected one?' Overlord asked, his voice weak.

'Yes,' Furan replied, nodding towards one of AWP's security forces. 'He is young and he looks strong. He should last longer than Collins did.'

'Yes, he will do for now,' Overlord said with a predatory smile.

Furan motioned to the guards and they grabbed the young soldier from the crowd of hostages and dragged him, struggling, to where Overlord was standing.

'Please, I'm getting married in three weeks. Please don't kill me,' the young man begged.

'You're wasting your time if you're trying to appeal to my humanity,' Overlord said with a sneer. 'You see, I haven't got any.'

Furan's communicator earpiece bleeped and he tapped it to initiate a connection, turning away as the first of the slimy black Animus tendrils burst from the skin on Overlord's forearm. He ignored the sounds of shock and then terror from the young soldier and the frantic, strangled gurgling that inevitably followed.

'Furan here. Go ahead.'

'Sir, we've just received word from our source that the US Navy think they've found Darkdoom's submarine,' the voice on the other end of the line reported.

'Where?'

'Off the coast of Spain. It appears to be heading for Britain,' the voice replied.

'They're sure it's Darkdoom?'

'Yes, sir. Nothing else could be moving as fast as this contact.'

'Excellent. Get me Raven.'

☢ ☢ ☢

The Professor looked up as Otto walked into the Megalodon's laboratory.

'Hello, Otto,' he said. 'Is there something I can do for you?'

'Yeah, I'm getting a few glitches with H.I.V.E.mind's vocal synthesis through this relay,' Otto said, placing the unit that the Professor had given him earlier on top of the workbench. 'I was wondering if you could take a look at it.'

'Of course,' the Professor replied. 'I'm afraid I rather rushed putting it together. I wouldn't be at all surprised if there's a few bugs.'

The Professor picked up the device and examined it for a few seconds before activating it. H.I.V.E.mind's face appeared on the screen.

'Do not do this, Otto,' H.I.V.E.mind said.

'Do not do wh—' was all the Professor had time to say before he felt a finger press into the soft flesh behind his ear and he lost consciousness. Otto laid him gently back in his chair and moved to the counter.

'You are acting in direct contravention of Doctor Nero's explicit instructions,' H.I.V.E.mind said.

'Yeah, and it's not like I've ever done *that* before,' Otto said sarcastically.

'This is not what I intended when I suggested that we attempt to interface directly with the Animus. We need to develop a safer method,' H.I.V.E.mind said.

'We don't have time for that and you know it,' Otto

said as he walked over to the small magnetic containment device that held the dormant Animus sample.

'You are putting yourself and everyone else on board this vessel at risk,' H.I.V.E.mind said calmly.

'It's going to work,' Otto replied as he pulled the metal tube from its stand and clipped it into a hypodermic injector gun. 'It has to.'

'Please, Otto,' H.I.V.E.mind said, 'there has to be another way.'

'Maybe, but I'm not really the cautious type,' Otto said with a slight smile before sticking the needle into his arm and pulling the trigger. He closed his eyes and waited. At first there was nothing but slowly he began to feel something stirring inside him, a slight tingle in his arm. He reached out with his abilities and tried to make contact with the waking Animus inside him. He could sense it, a cold alien presence, already beginning the process of replication, preparing to take control of its host.

'Do you feel it?' Otto whispered.

'Yes,' H.I.V.E.mind replied, 'though I am struggling to make sense of any of the data encoded within it.'

'Let me translate,' Otto said, forcing a connection with the simple, almost animal consciousness of the Animus. He had spent months trapped inside his own body listening to the digital hiss of the previous generation of Animus that had once coursed through him. This was different though, simpler, not as filled with an instinctive loathing for organic life as the previous generation had been.

'I have accessed the core code,' H.I.V.E.mind reported. 'It will take me a few seconds to analyse its command structure and implant new instructions.'

'Quickly, please,' Otto said as he began to feel the first hints of something eating away at his conscious mind, subverting his free will. He tried hard not to think about all that he had been forced to do when that had happened before, the lives that had been lost.

'Upload complete,' H.I.V.E.mind reported. 'Command rewrite in progress.'

Otto nodded, gritting his teeth and fighting to stay conscious. There was a horrifying sensation of countless alien voices whispering inside his skull, all trying to get him to release control, to sleep.

'Not this time,' he gasped. He started to squeeze the trigger on the injector gun. The injection chamber was empty and if he pulled the trigger the air bubble that would enter his bloodstream would travel straight to his brain. At least it would be quick.

Suddenly he sensed a change. The Animus was no longer replicating and the hissing inside his skull diminished and was gone.

'I think it worked,' he said quietly.

'It would appear so,' H.I.V.E.mind said. 'I suggest that we remove it from your body as quickly as possible.'

'You read my mind,' Otto replied.

'No, I did not,' H.I.V.E.mind replied. 'Your neural architecture is too sophisticated for me to translate patterns of synaptic firing into a coherent –'

'It's a figure of speech,' Otto said with a tired smile. The Professor groaned and stirred slightly in his seat. Otto went over and gently shook his uninjured shoulder. The old man's eyes slowly opened and a fleeting look of confusion on his face was quickly replaced by a frown.

'Tell me you didn't do what I think you did,' the Professor said.

'I did,' Otto replied. 'The Animus has been encoded with new instructions.'

'Where is it?' the Professor asked.

'Here,' Otto said, tapping his own chest. 'Get the containment vessel ready.'

The Professor nodded and got to work preparing the magnetic field generator. Otto took a deep breath and gave the Animus inside him a new instruction.

'I think this is going to hurt,' he said as he held out his arm, his fingers curling into a fist. Something dark suddenly appeared, squirming beneath the skin of his forearm. Otto hissed in sudden pain as the Animus punched through the skin of his arm and slithered towards his hand. He picked up the small metal cylinder and held his fingertip over its open end. The Animus slid down his finger and fell into the cylinder.

'Now the fun part,' Otto said with a crooked smile as he sealed the cylinder and placed it into the magnetic containment device.

'And what would that be?' Professor Pike said, while checking that the containment field was functioning properly.

'Now we get to tell Doctor Nero that we did exactly what he explicitly told us not to do,' Otto replied.

'You, Mr Malpense,' the Professor replied, shaking his head slightly, 'have a very strange definition of fun.'

☻ ☻ ☻

'Of all the stupid, crazy, hare-brained things!' Laura said, punching Otto in the chest.

'You forgot irresponsible,' Otto replied with a smile.

'And what did he have to say about all this?' Lucy said, nodding towards Dr Nero, who was standing on the other side of the Megalodon's command centre.

'Something about not knowing whether he should shake my hand or have me shot,' Otto replied. 'To be honest, I think he's still trying to decide.'

'I'm just glad you're OK,' Lucy said, 'you bloody idiot.'

'I agree,' Wing said. 'With the idiot part, that is.'

'At least now we have a way to save anyone Overlord used that stuff on,' Laura said. 'I wouldn't mind having Raven back on our team.'

'If we can find her,' Wing remarked.

'I'm slightly more worried about her finding us at the moment, to be honest,' Shelby said. 'If we do meet up with her again I'd like to volunteer Otto for the whole injecting her with something against her will assignment.'

'Yes, that may prove somewhat *problematic*,' Wing said, raising an eyebrow. 'For now we have other concerns though. I assume you have all reviewed the briefing materials that Doctor Nero provided?'

'Yeah, it looks pretty straightforward,' Shelby said, 'at least in comparison to the usual suicide missions we end up on.'

'Hey, guys,' Nigel said as he and Franz walked into the room. 'My dad told me that you're all leaving for a while. Nothing too dangerous, I hope?'

'Nah, we'll be back before you know it,' Shelby said.

'I am thinking that I have been hearing this before,' Franz said, 'usually just before there is the shooting and exploding.'

'Well, maybe this time will be different,' Shelby replied.

'Torpedoes in the water!' one of Darkdoom's men shouted from the other side of the command centre.

'Or maybe not.'

'Launch countermeasures!' Captain Sanders ordered. 'Sonar, who's shooting at us?'

'I have a Virginia class attack submarine, sir – correction, two Virginia class subs three miles off our port bow.'

'Countermeasures away!'

'Where the hell did they come from?' Sanders said angrily.

'They were waiting for us, sir. They must have been dead in the water for our sonar not to have picked them up.'

'The first two torps have switched targets to the decoys,' one of the weapons officers reported. 'I have four more inbound.'

'Initiate evasive manoeuvres,' Sanders barked, 'and plot me a course away from those boats.'

'Are we going to be able to make the drop point, Captain?' Darkdoom asked quickly.

'Not with those hunter-killers on us, sir,' the Captain replied. 'If we surface with them in range we'll be sitting ducks. Our only hope is to outrun them. You can bet that half the US Navy ships in the North Atlantic are on their way here now.'

'Very well,' Darkdoom said calmly. 'Prep the Hammerhead for launch.'

'Aye aye, sir,' the Captain replied with a nod.

'It would seem that Overlord has enlisted the help of

the American Navy,' Nero said, the deck tilting beneath his feet as the Megalodon's helmsman threw it into a series of evasive turns.

'Yes,' Darkdoom replied, 'and I'm sure we can both guess why.' He glanced over to where Otto was standing with the other Alphas.

'We have a torp tracking past the countermeasures,' the weapons officer shouted. 'Brace for impact!'

There was a sudden crashing thud from somewhere outside the Megalodon's hull and the whole vessel shuddered.

'Detonation fifty metres off the port bow.'

'They've set their fuses for proximity detonation,' Sanders said.

'They're trying to force us to surface,' Darkdoom replied, 'not sink us. Max, you have to take your team and get out of here now. Go down to the launch bay and take my mini-sub. You should be able to slip away undetected if we time this right. I'll meet back up with you at the rendezvous point in the States.'

'I'll see you there,' Nero said. 'Are you sure you'll be able to get clear?'

'Oh, don't worry – the Megalodon has a few tricks up her sleeve yet,' Darkdoom replied with a smile. Nero shook Darkdoom's hand and strode over to the group of worried-looking Alphas.

'Nigel, Franz, you stay here,' he said as the sound of another nearby explosion sent a shudder through the hull. 'The rest of you, with me.'

Darkdoom watched as Nero and his students ran out of the command centre.

'Launch Hydra torpedoes, full spread, both targets,' Darkdoom ordered. 'It's time we showed our American friends what happens when someone shoots at the Megalodon.'

☢ ☢ ☢

'Torpedo, torpedo, torpedo!' the crew member manning the USS *Texas'* sonar station yelled. 'I have six . . . seven . . . no, eight fish in the water and heading this way.'

'Launch decoys,' the Captain shouted.

'Decoys away!'

'We have negative tracking on incoming warheads,' the weapons officer shouted. 'Their torps are ignoring our countermeasures.'

'Oh my God!' the sonar officer said quietly.

'What is it, sonar?' the Captain demanded impatiently.

'Incoming torpedoes have separated. I have sixty-four incoming tracks.'

The Captain felt his blood run cold.

'How many?'

'Sixty-four, sir,' the sonar operator said with a nervous gulp. 'It looks like their torpedoes have launched smaller secondary sub-munitions.'

'Evasive manoeuvres!' the Captain yelled, already knowing that it would do no good.

'They've launched on the *North Carolina*,' the comms officer reported. 'They're reporting that their counter-measures were completely ineffective too.'

The *Texas* and *North Carolina* were two of the most advanced submarines on the planet but the mysterious boat out there was making them look like tinker toys. He braced himself as he watched the swarm of incoming contacts on the sonar screen.

'Transmit details of that thing's weaponry to Atlantic command,' the Captain said, 'while we still can.'

☢ ☢ ☢

Otto and the others ran up the boarding ramp of the compact submarine that hung above the launch hatch in the belly of the Megalodon.

'Nero and his team are on board,' the Hammerhead's helmsman reported as Nero took the seat next to him and put on a comms headset. Otto and the others quickly strapped themselves into the seats behind him. 'I'm buttoning us up. Crash-flood the launch chamber on my mark.'

The hatch behind Otto whirred shut with a solid thunk.

'Three . . . two . . . one . . . mark!'

There was a rumbling sound as thousands of gallons of seawater flooded the chamber outside. After a few seconds the noise decreased and all the passengers could hear was a gentle creaking from the hull.

'This is Darkdoom,' a voice said over the speakers. 'Hydra torpedo detonation in ten seconds. Prepare to launch.'

Otto realised that he was holding his breath.

'Launch now!'

The helmsman smacked a switch on the instrument panel and the Hammerhead dropped through the open doors below, diving away below the Megalodon at the precise moment that the swarm of warheads from the Hydras detonated. Through the thick toughened glass of the cockpit window they saw hundreds of explosions light up the darkened depths of the ocean several miles away. Otto gave a low whistle.

'Darkdoom doesn't believe in doing things by halves, does he?' he said.

'Despite appearances the intention is not to destroy our pursuers, just temporarily blind and confuse them. Let us hope that the distraction was enough to cover our departure,' Nero said.

'Megalodon to Hammerhead,' Darkdoom's voice came

over the comms system. 'We are heading out at full speed. Let's see if the Americans aren't too stunned to give chase.'

'Understood,' Nero replied. 'Good luck.'

'You too,' Darkdoom said and the line went dead.

'And now,' Nero said quietly, staring out into the black water surrounding them, 'we wait.'

☢ ☢ ☢

The Captain of the USS *Texas* climbed to his feet, his ears still ringing from the massive detonation just a few seconds earlier.

'Damage report!' he barked.

'A handful of minor injuries, sir,' one of his crewmen replied, 'but no major structural damage.'

'Target is moving away at – well, frankly impossible speed,' another member of the crew reported. The Captain couldn't understand it – their target had a tiny sonar signature and was too fast for anything bigger than a torpedo and yet it had just launched a spread of warheads that even the *Texas* could not hope to match.

'Lay in a pursuit course,' the Captain snapped. 'Signal the *North Carolina* to accompany us and relay the target's track to Atlantic Command. Tell them we need every ship they can spare. I'm damned if I'm letting this fish slip the net.'

The Hammerhead surfaced next to the deserted jetty, moonlight reflecting off her glistening black hull. The hatch in the side of the submarine slid open and Nero climbed down on to the wooden pier, looking around for any sign that their arrival might have been spotted. Seeing nothing, he gestured for his students to follow him.

'This is where we part ways,' he said, looking at the assembled Alphas. 'There is a village five kilometres up the coast where you should be able to *borrow* some transport. I'm sure I don't need to remind you that you should avoid any entanglements with local law enforcement.'

'What, you mean that five kids in identical uniforms jacking a car in the middle of the night isn't normal around here?' Shelby asked.

'Just try to be discreet,' Nero said, raising an eyebrow. 'As soon as you are mobile, head for GCHQ, but do not try to enter the facility until I call you on this.' He passed a mobile phone to Otto. 'Stick to the plan and remember your training. You are one of the most capable groups of students I have ever trained and I know you won't let me down. Just be careful.'

'Yes, sir,' Otto replied. 'We'll try to avoid blowing anything up.'

'How very reassuring,' Nero said with a slight smile. 'I'll

see you all again soon. Good luck.'

With that he turned and walked away into the night.

'I must admit that I am somewhat surprised that Doctor Nero is allowing us to tackle this mission without an escort,' Wing said after a few seconds.

'Yeah,' Shelby said. 'How does he know we won't just run? H.I.V.E. isn't exactly a holiday camp, after all.'

'I'd like to think it's because he trusts us,' Laura replied.

'Maybe,' Otto said, putting his equipment pack on his back, 'or it could just be that he knows that in a world where Overlord isn't stopped there'll be nowhere left to run to.'

☢ ☢ ☢

'Right. Who's driving?' Shelby said as she opened the door of the 4 X 4.

'Not Laura,' Otto said with a cheeky grin.

'OK, OK, so the holographic training sessions haven't gone brilliantly,' Laura said, holding her hands up. 'There's no need to go on about it.'

'Remind me,' Otto replied, 'how many pedestrians did you kill last time?'

'Twelve,' Laura said quietly, 'but they were only holograms.'

'Tell that to their poor holographic families,' Shelby said with a grin.

'May I suggest that Mr Fanchu drives,' H.I.V.E.mind said, his vocal transmitter clipped to Otto's chest. 'I believe that his appearance is the least likely to draw unwanted attention.'

'Since when is height an indication of driving ability?' Otto said.

'You getting jealous, shorty?' Shelby said with a grin.

'I am happy to do it if it will ensure an uneventful journey,' Wing said.

'I don't really care as long as it's not Roadkill Brand,' Shelby said, putting her arm around Laura's shoulder. 'Take the wheel, big guy.'

They all climbed into the car, with Otto taking the front passenger seat.

'Otto, would you be so kind,' Wing said, gesturing towards the dashboard. Otto closed his eyes and connected with the car's electronic ignition system, quickly persuading it that it really should start the engine.

'H.I.V.E. road trip!' Shelby said happily. 'Let's roll!'

Otto punched the location of GCHQ into the car's onboard satnav as Wing gently accelerated away down the road.

'How long's it going to take us to get there?' Lucy asked. The first signs of sunrise were now visible on the horizon.

'About two and a half hours,' Otto said, studying the display mounted in the dashboard.

'Cool,' Shelby said. 'Altogether now! One hundred bottles of beer hanging on the wall, one hundred bottles of beer . . .'

'It may seem longer though,' Otto said with a sigh.

chapter seven

Nero sank into one of the comfortable leather chairs as the secretary behind the desk on the other side of the room threw a curious glance in his direction. Clearly she was not used to someone getting to see her boss quite so easily. Nero smiled back at her.

'He's just finishing his current meeting,' she said politely. 'He'll be with you in a minute.'

'Excellent,' Nero replied, 'and thank you again for the tea.'

He took a sip from the fine china cup. One of the small pleasures of returning to England, he thought to himself.

'Three months!' the angry-looking man said as he stormed out of the adjoining office. 'Three months it took to set up that meeting, and he just asks us to leave after five minutes because "something's come up". I don't believe it!'

'I do hope that I haven't caused too much disruption,'

Nero said to the secretary as he watched the furious man leave.

'Not at all,' the secretary replied. 'He's ready for you now. You can go in.'

'Thank you,' Nero said as he stood up and headed through the door.

The man behind the heavy wooden desk in the centre of the book-lined room stood up as Nero entered, gesturing for him to take a seat in one of the sofas on either side of the fireplace.

'Thank you for seeing me at such short notice, Prime Minister,' Nero said. 'I appreciate you sparing the time.'

'How could I refuse a request from my former head-master?' the Prime Minister said with a crooked smile. 'Tell me, how is the old place?'

'Not much has changed,' Nero said. 'Though you appear to have done quite well for yourself since you left us.'

Duncan Cavendish had been one of Nero's most promising students when he left H.I.V.E. twenty years ago. Nero had always known he would do well in the outside world and Cavendish had not disappointed him.

'Well, after the unfortunate display by the former leader of the opposition at their conference a few years ago it was difficult for the general public to take his party seriously.

Dropping your trousers in front of the TV cameras has that effect sometimes.'

'Would you believe me if I told you that one of my current students was responsible for that?' Nero said with a smile.

'Actually, that wouldn't surprise me at all,' Cavendish replied. 'Do be sure to thank them for me.'

'Of course,' Nero said. 'I'm just glad that details of your education have remained secret.'

'You taught me all about the art of the cover-up – just one of many lessons that have helped me in my new career. You know, I still remember what you said to me on the day you transferred me from the Political and Financial stream to the Alphas. *The best way to manipulate is to lead.* I may use it as the title of my memoirs.' Cavendish laughed.

'Perhaps a little too honest,' Nero said, smiling.

'Maybe. Now tell me, what can I do for you?'

'I assume that you know about recent developments at the Americans' Advanced Weapons Project facility?' Nero said.

'Not as much as you might think,' Cavendish replied. 'Our cousins across the water have been surprisingly unforthcoming. The boys at MI6 tell me that there's been some sort of terrorist attack and we've lost touch with a couple of our military brass who were attending a demonstration there. That and the fact that half of their Atlantic fleet seems to be heading for the Channel have made me rather keen to speak to the President. Unfortunately, he's been unavailable for the past forty-eight hours. I'm afraid that the Special Relationship is often a one-way street on these occasions. I take it that there's more to it than we know?'

'I'm afraid so,' Nero replied. 'I can't go into too much detail but I need your help.'

'With what?'

'I have a team heading to GCHQ. I need you to grant them access to Echelon.'

'I see,' Cavendish said, frowning slightly. 'May I ask why?'

'I'm afraid I can't tell you,' Nero replied. 'Suffice to say the nature of the threat we are facing is global in scope.'

'The situation in America is that serious?'

'Yes. H.I.V.E. has been taken and the ruling council captured. G.L.O.V.E. is in disarray and we may be all that stands between the man who's in control of the AWP facility and global domination. This is our last chance. You know that I wouldn't ask this of you unless it was absolutely necessary.'

'I'll inform GCHQ to give them unrestricted access,' Cavendish said, suddenly looking worried. 'Is there anything else that I can do?'

'Yes. I need a civilian transport to the States, the fastest you can find.'

'That shouldn't be a problem.'

'Thank you. I know how much I am asking. You didn't have to do this.'

'Yes, I did. You were never a man prone to exaggeration. I'll make the calls.'

☢ ☢ ☢

'Should I pull over?' Wing said, glancing at the blue flashing lights in the rear-view mirror.

'The maximum speed of the pursuing vehicle is considerably higher than our own,' H.I.V.E.mind replied. 'Attempted flight would also considerably increase the chances of attracting more law enforcement personnel.'

'Doesn't sound like we've got much choice,' Otto said, twisting in his seat and looking back at the police car that was rapidly catching up with them.

'But we're so close!' Laura said. They were only ten kilometres from GCHQ and now, suddenly, it looked like they might not make it at all.

'We're not done yet,' Lucy said as Wing pulled the car over to the side of the quiet country road. 'Let me talk to them.'

Lucy opened the passenger door and stepped down as the police car pulled up ten metres behind them. The two officers in the car leapt out and advanced towards her.

'Driver, out of the car, now!' the first officer shouted.

'Is there something wrong, Officer?' Lucy asked innocently.

'Yes, miss. You and your friends are in possession of a stolen vehicle. Driver, step out of the vehicle – we won't ask again,' the second policeman said, extending his baton with a flick of the wrist. Wing got out of the car slowly.

'I think there's been some kind of misunderstanding, Officers,' Lucy said, smiling sweetly. 'You see, *this car isn't stolen.*'

The two policemen stopped in their tracks, looking slightly confused.

'Why did we stop you again?' one of them asked Lucy, looking genuinely puzzled.

'I don't know,' Lucy replied, 'but if I were you I'd *give me your car keys and go and have a nice long sleep in the bushes over there.*'

The policemen looked for a moment like they didn't understand and then one of them reached into his pocket and handed her the keys.

'Thanks,' Lucy said, watching as the pair of them turned and walked silently off into the bushes at the side of the road.

'Dexter, I could kiss you,' Shelby said as Lucy climbed

back into the car. 'If Otto doesn't mind, that is?'

'Oh, just ignore her. That was nice work, Lucy,' Laura said.

'Shall we get moving?' Otto asked, restarting the car with a mental nudge.

'Is it just me or does this car seem to be getting smaller?' Wing said under his breath.

'I am curious,' H.I.V.E.mind said. 'Is it normal for friends to attempt to cause each other emotional discomfort in this way?'

'Welcome to our world,' Laura said with a chuckle, shaking her head.

Suddenly the mobile phone in Otto's pocket started to ring.

'Hello,' he said, holding it to his ear.

'Mr Malpense,' Dr Nero replied, 'I have got you the access you require. How far out from GCHQ are you?'

'Ten minutes,' Otto said, glancing at the satnav display.

'Good. The code word you need to get past the guards at the gate is Tsunami. They have been told to expect your arrival.'

'Got it,' Otto replied.

'Please let me know when you've transmitted the signal,' Nero said. 'I'm on my way to pick you up. ETA forty minutes.'

'Understood. I'll call you when we're done.'

Otto ended the call and turned to speak to the others.

'We're all clear,' he said. 'Nero's on his way.'

☣ ☣ ☣

Duncan Cavendish pulled his mobile phone from his pocket and punched in a number. He waited a couple of seconds before there was an answer.

'Sign in, please,' a computerised voice replied.

'Disciple Nine,' Cavendish said. 'Get me Furan.'

'Voice print confirmed, transfer in progress.'

The line was silent then a voice on the other end replied.

'Furan here.'

'It's Cavendish,' he replied. 'I've just had a visit from Nero. The Malpense boy is heading for the GCHQ building in Cheltenham.'

'Excellent. I shall inform Raven immediately,' Furan replied. 'Do you know what they want at GCHQ?'

'Access to Echelon.'

'Did Nero say why?'

'No, he wouldn't tell me.'

'They probably want more information about what is happening at the facility in America,' Furan said.

'I could have them taken into custody at the gates if you want,' Cavendish suggested.

'No, give them access,' Furan replied. 'They will only find out what the Americans know already and that will not help them. Leave the boy's retrieval to Raven. I don't want to spook Malpense. If he senses something is wrong and runs we could lose him.'

'If Raven is going to take the boy at GCHQ I need it to look like a terrorist attack. Anything else might raise too many difficult questions.'

'I'm sure that Natalya will be able to come up with something,' Furan replied, and the line went dead.

☺ ☺ ☺

Otto and the others travelled the remaining distance to the GCHQ gates in silence. A long straight road led to the outer perimeter fence and the gatehouse at the end of it was manned by several heavily armed guards. Otto tried to ignore the assault rifles that were trained on them as they approached. Wing pulled up at the assigned spot and one of the guards walked over to the car as Otto lowered the window.

'Good morning, sir,' the guard said, the polite greeting at odds with his stern expression.

'Tsunami,' Otto said, and the guard nodded.

'We've been expecting you,' he replied. 'Please proceed through the gate and follow the security vehicle to the main building.' Otto closed the window as the heavy security barrier lowered into the ground in front of them. Wing dropped into formation behind the military vehicle and followed it towards the large doughnut-shaped building that was the hub of Britain's intelligence communications network.

'Big place,' Lucy said as they rolled towards the main doors.

'Lots of people to eavesdrop on,' Otto said, finding it hard to shake the sensation that they were walking into the lion's den. The vehicle they were following came to a stop and one of the guards that climbed down from it motioned for them to step out of the car.

'This way, please,' he said, indicating the large doors.

Otto and the others walked inside the building and took in their surroundings. The large glass-walled entrance area was patrolled by armed guards and surveillance cameras seemed to be mounted in every corner. Long channels leading further into the building were fitted with numerous different types of electronic scanners. Smuggling anything through would be next to impossible. Otto was suddenly very glad that they had not needed to try and infiltrate the building. Even with the unique skills that he and his friends possessed he could see that it would have been extremely difficult.

A short, balding man in a badly fitting suit walked down the entrance channel towards them. He had the air of someone who was being told to do something that he really did not want to do.

'If you'll come with me, please,' the man said. 'My name is Colin Reynolds and I'll be your escort while you're here. I've been informed of what you need – heaven only knows what they're thinking in London but ours is not to reason why.'

'Thanks,' Otto said. 'Don't worry, we'll be gone before you know it.'

'Yes, well, let's head inside, shall we?' Reynolds said, looking irritated.

'Lead the way,' Otto replied with a smile that he secretly hoped would annoy the officious bureaucrat even more. As they all followed Reynolds through the entry channel a buzzer sounded.

'Do you have any electronic devices on you?' he asked.

'Just a mobile phone and this,' Otto said, holding out H.I.V.E.mind's vocal transmitter.

'And what is that?' Reynolds said, eyeing the device suspiciously.

'It's my . . . er . . . MP3 player,' Otto lied.

'Well, you'll have to leave them here, I'm afraid,' Reynolds said. 'We've been instructed to grant you access but nobody is allowed beyond this point with unsecured electronic devices. No exceptions. You can pick them up on your way out.'

'Fair enough,' Otto said, trying hard not to smile If Reynolds really knew what he could do or what he had rattling around inside his skull, he'd probably have a heart attack. Otto had everything he needed with him and no one could take it from him.

They passed through the rest of the scanners in the channel without incident and Reynolds led them further inside the huge edifice. As with most buildings used by the intelligence services there was actually very little to see beyond firmly closed office doors and signs pointing to other departments that were identified by meaningless numbers. After walking down numerous identical anonymous corridors Reynolds finally led them to an elevator that was flanked by two heavily armed guards.

'In you go,' he said with a sniff. 'I'm not cleared beyond this point.'

'Thanks, Colin,' Otto said with a smile. 'I'd tell you why we're here but . . . it's classified.' Otto actually thought he might burst out laughing as Reynolds glared at him and then stormed off down the corridor muttering to himself.

'Be nice,' Lucy said, elbowing him in the ribs as they stepped into the lift. 'We're trying not to upset anyone, remember.'

'Sorry,' Otto said, grinning. 'Couldn't resist.'

The elevator descended for what seemed like an

unusually long time before the doors slid open and the Alphas found themselves in a long windowless corridor ending in a single door flanked by two more armed guards. Above it was a single word.

Echelon.

As they approached one of the guards punched a code into the numeric keypad mounted on the wall and the door hissed open. Inside dozens of technicians sat at consoles monitoring hundreds of screens. A woman with curly blonde hair wearing jeans and a T-shirt walked over to them and inspected them carefully.

'Could you give me the code word, please?' she asked.

'Tsunami,' Otto said, trying to ignore the background hum of digital activity that surrounded him.

'Welcome to Echelon,' the woman said with a smile. 'I've been instructed to give you full access. I've prepared a terminal in one of the side offices. If you'd like to come with me . . .'

Otto and the others followed her into the small room off to one side of the main monitoring area, which contained a single desk with an array of touch screens mounted on its surface.

'I'm not sure exactly what it is that you need,' the woman said. 'I'm told that you'll know what to do. If there's anything you want or if you require help at all, I'll be just outside.'

'Thanks,' Otto said. 'I think we'll be OK.'

'Fine. I'll leave you to it.'

She left the office, closing the door behind her. As she walked back out on to the main floor one of her colleagues looked up at her with a curious expression.

'What's that all about?' the man asked, nodding towards the office.

'Don't know, don't want to know,' the woman said with a slight shake of her head, 'but considering who my orders came from I'm guessing that it's a little bit above our pay grade.'

'But they're just kids,' the man said, looking puzzled.

'Kids with a higher security clearance than you, Mike,' the woman said with a shrug, heading back to her desk.

Back inside the office Otto looked at the array of monitors on the desk with a mixture of excitement and apprehension. If there was a pot of gold that lay at the end of the signals intelligence rainbow, this was it. Echelon may have been a badly kept secret within the intelligence community but to most members of the general public it was still just a myth. At its core it was nothing more than an advanced search engine but what made it astonishing was the amount of data that it filtered. Every phone call, internet search or radio transmission was routed through the Echelon servers, where intelligent algorithms scanned through their content looking for key phrases of interest. It was a giant ear listening to the whole of humanity and highlighting to its operators anything that might be of concern to them. Otto thought there was something deeply sinister about it – it represented a huge invasion of privacy for people all over the world. For his money it was just as evil as anything that he'd seen G.L.O.V.E. or any of their foes produce.

'He who sacrifices freedom for security deserves neither,' he said under his breath.

'What's that?' Laura asked.

'Nothing – just something an old revolutionary once said,' Otto replied. 'Check this out.'

He pointed to a series of diagnostic readouts on one of the screens.

'I can't believe the bandwidth they're dealing with here,' Laura said, studying the monitors with an expression of awe.

'It's the level of real-time decryption I can't believe,' Otto replied.

'What bit level of encryption before they hit processing bottlenecks, do you reckon? They have to be using a massively parallel array,' Laura said.

'The who do what now?' Shelby said with a sigh.

'They're talking computer at each other again, aren't they,' Lucy said, sitting down in one of the chairs against the wall.

'I believe they prefer the term nerdspeak,' Wing replied as Otto and Laura chatted away to one another, seemingly oblivious to the rest of the world.

'Er . . . guys,' Shelby said, stifling a laugh, 'hate to break up the party but we're on the clock here.' She tapped on her watch.

'Yeah, I suppose we'd better get on with this,' Otto said with a sigh. 'Can you clear me routers on every major transmission hub?'

'On it,' Laura said, tapping away at one of the touch screens.

'Right. You ready, H.I.V.E.mind?' Otto asked.

I am ready, the voice in Otto's head replied.

'OK, I'm going to hook us up.' Otto explained. 'Once I'm connected to each server I'll give you the word and you can begin transmission.'

Understood.

'I know you can't tell me what this signal is,' Otto said, 'but tell me one thing before we do this.'

What do you want to know?

'Why does it have to be transmitted from here?' Otto asked.

Because this is the only place on Earth where we can be sure that the transmission will not be intercepted. The identities of the recipients of this transmission must not be discovered and the only way we can be certain that they remain hidden is if we send the signal to them directly from here. Echelon monitors every other network that is sufficiently powerful to send the signal. G.L.O.V.E.net would have been both secure and powerful enough but H.I.V.E. is the hub of that network.'

'I get it,' Otto said, suddenly understanding. 'When we lost H.I.V.E. we lost the network that was supposed to send this message. Any other network would have been vulnerable to Echelon and the only way around that is to take advantage of the fact that the one thing Echelon can't hear is its own voice.'

That is correct.

Otto found himself wondering again what this signal could be. What was it that Nero had to be so sure would not be intercepted by anyone? It wasn't that H.I.V.E.mind wouldn't tell him, it was that it *couldn't* tell him. It was built into his code, part of his fundamental architecture. If there was one thing that Otto hated it was not knowing what was going on.

'OK,' Laura said, 'routers are clear.'

'Here goes nothing,' Otto said, closing his eyes.

The connection he made was instant and over-whelming. For just a split second he felt as though he was suddenly spread throughout billions of different places all over the world at the same instant. He could see every-thing, hear everything. It was the most fascinating and yet horrifying thing he had ever experienced. At that instant he made a decision, something that he simply had to do.

Connection verified. Target locations confirmed. Transmission initiated, H.I.V.E.mind said.

Otto tried to ignore the bewildering sensation of near omnipotence and instead focus on his task. He began to build blocks of code in his head, transmitting them as quickly as he could. He consciously hid what he was doing from H.I.V.E.mind – no one could know what he was planning.

Transmission complete, H.I.V.E.mind said.

Otto needed just a few more seconds.

You may disconnect, H.I.V.E.mind said.

Otto fired off the last block of his own code.

Otto, you may disconnect now, H.I.V.E.mind repeated.

'Done,' Otto gasped, disconnecting from Echelon's network and feeling a sudden wave of dizziness. He grabbed the edge of the desk to stop himself from falling as the room spun around him. Wing caught him and helped him down into one of the nearby chairs.

'Are you all right, my friend?' he asked, studying Otto's unusually pale face.

'I'm fine,' Otto said, taking a deep breath. 'That was just a bit much to take in. Unless anyone has any objections I'd like to get the hell out of here. This place gives me the creeps.'

☉ ☉ ☉

Nero looked out of the window of the helicopter as it flew low over the English countryside. Not for the first time in the past couple of days he found himself wondering if he had done the right thing. He had always known that the plan he had put in motion might be necessary one day but, that didn't make him any more comfortable with the possible consequences.

'We're two minutes out,' the pilot reported and Nero just nodded. Moments later the cell phone in his inside pocket began to ring and he quickly took the call.

'Hello, Mr Malpense,' Nero said. 'I hope you have good news.'

'Yes,' Otto replied. 'H.I.V.E.mind has sent the signal. Any chance of you telling me what this is all about now?'

'All in good time, Mr Malpense,' Nero replied. 'I take it that you received full cooperation from the GCHQ staff?'

'Yeah, though I think they might be wondering why a bunch of kids in jumpsuits were given access to the most secure data network on the planet.'

'No doubt. Let's hope that they never find out,' Nero said. 'I shall be there very shortly. Are you ready to leave?'

'Yes, we're inside the main entrance.'

'I'll be on the ground in thirty seconds,' Nero said as they crossed GCHQ's perimeter fence, heading for the helipad a short distance from the entrance.

'OK, see you in a minute,' Otto said and the line went dead.

The helicopter was on its final approach when the front entrance of the GCHQ building suddenly exploded in an enormous ball of fire.

'What the hell –' the pilot said, staring at the billowing cloud of smoke that shrouded the front of the building. Nero watched in horror as something blew away the cloud, revealing the huge hole torn in the entrance. There was a shimmer in the air and he felt his heart sink as a Shroud dropship uncloaked, landing just twenty metres from the building. The rear hatch opened and a figure dressed in black ran down the boarding ramp, pulling two glowing purple swords from the crossed sheaths on her back. A squad of heavily armed men followed close behind her.

'Get me down there now!' Nero shouted.

☻ ☻ ☻

Raven ran through the smouldering rubble, swords drawn, searching for her target. The glass frontage of GCHQ was supposed to be bombproof but the Shroud's missile strike had torn it apart.

'Fan out. Find the boy,' she snapped at the soldiers accompanying her. 'He's here somewhere.'

There was a groan from nearby and Laura sat up, still

dazed from the explosion. Raven signalled to two of the soldiers to take her.

'Put her on board the Shroud – she may be useful.'

Raven watched as the two men dragged the struggling girl away before turning her attention back to the ruined room. Through the clouds of dust hanging in the air she could just make out another figure in a black jumpsuit staggering through the remains of the entrance area. She moved quickly towards the figure and saw that it was Lucy Dexter, bleeding from a gash on her forehead. As she saw Raven approaching, Lucy took a couple of stumbling steps backwards, a look of startled fear on her face.

'*Leave me al—*' Lucy never had time to finish the sentence as Raven clamped her hand over her mouth.

'Not this time,' Raven said, wrapping her arm round Lucy's throat and squeezing until she felt the girl lose consciousness. She called two of the soldiers over.

'Put her on board too. Make sure she's sedated,' Raven said. The soldiers picked up Lucy's unconscious body and carried it outside. There was the sudden sound of gunfire from outside as the GCHQ security forces started to recover from the shock and mount a counter-attack. Raven continued to move through the rubble – she needed to find Malpense fast. She almost tripped over the body lying on the floor half covered in debris, the white hair at the back of his head stained red with blood.

Kneeling down, she placed two fingers on Otto's neck and felt a strong pulse. She quickly searched his pockets and found what looked like a partly dismantled Blackbox and a mobile phone, then flung them against the nearest wall, smashing them to pieces. Satisfied that they could no longer be tracked she pulled Otto from under the fallen plasterwork and slung his limp body over her shoulder.

'Raven to all forces. I have acquired the primary target. Everyone back on board the Shroud now!' she said quickly into her throat mic. She ran through the doors towards the waiting dropship and pounded up the boarding ramp, lowering Otto carefully on to the deck.

'Pilot, get us out of here,' Raven said and the Shroud's idling engines roared into life. She looked back towards the entrance as the Shroud lifted from the ground and saw Wing running through the debris towards her. He leapt into the air as the Shroud climbed, just catching the edge of the boarding ramp, and started to pull himself inside. Raven took two steps towards him as he tried to haul himself up over the edge and kicked him in the jaw. Wing's head snapped back and he dropped off the loading ramp and fell. He hit the ground hard, landing on his side with a thud.

'Wing!' Shelby shouted as she ran across the forecourt towards him. She rolled him on to his back and after a couple of seconds his eyes opened.

'Help me up,' he groaned, grabbing her shoulder and pulling himself to his feet. They both watched helplessly as the Shroud climbed into the sky, its loading ramp closing as the rounds from the GCHQ guards' assault rifles pinged harmlessly off its armoured hull. A moment later the skin of the dropship seemed to shimmer for a second and then it vanished from view as its cloaking field activated. Shelby turned as she heard footsteps running up behind her. It was Nero, flanked by several of the facility's security guards.

'Are you OK?' Nero asked.

'No, it was Raven,' Shelby said. 'She took Otto.'

'Laura and Lucy were also taken,' Wing said. 'Shelby and I were trapped by fallen debris when the explosion happened. By the time I managed to free us it was too late. I was too slow.'

'There was nothing you could have done,' Nero said. 'They took us completely by surprise.'

Nero looked at the scene of chaos and destruction. In the distance he could hear the wail of sirens as the first ambulances and fire engines arrived at the gates. He cursed himself for his stupidity. He had assumed that they had moved too quickly and quietly for Raven to have tracked them here. He should have known better than to underestimate her. Nero was tired of being one step behind Overlord and his plans. He hated to admit it, but at the moment he was being outplayed.

'What do we do now?' Shelby asked sadly.

Nero knew that there was only one place Raven could be heading. Overlord would want Otto brought to him immediately.

'Now, Miss Trinity,' he said, a note of grim determination in his voice, 'we take the fight to them.'

chapter eight

Overlord stared at his reflection in the mirror with a mixture of frustration and disgust. The body he had taken just a few hours before was already starting to fail. Soon he would no longer be able to take over humans without destroying them almost immediately. If he had not found a solution by then he might be trapped within the Animus for all eternity, incapable of communicating with anyone or anything. He cursed his original creators every day for denying him the ability to interface with other machines. The abilities that he had engineered into Otto at birth were now the one way he would ever be able to control those machines. Only then would he truly be able to remake this world in his image.

He turned away from the mirror and walked out of the room, heading for the laboratory that housed the most critical component of the next phase of his plan. Furan suddenly appeared, striding down the corridor towards him.

'Raven just reported in,' Furan said with a smile as he approached. 'She has Malpense. She'll be here in a few hours.'

'Excellent,' Overlord said with a smile. 'Make sure everything else is ready. We will proceed as soon as they arrive.'

'I will inform our technicians to prepare for release,' Furan said with a nod.

'Nothing can stop us now,' Overlord replied. 'The endgame begins.'

☸ ☸ ☸

Otto woke up, his head throbbing. He was handcuffed to the seat in the passenger compartment of a Shroud and sitting shackled to the seats opposite him were Laura and Lucy. Lucy was unconscious, her head tipped back against the bulkhead, but Laura was awake.

'Hey,' Otto whispered. 'Where are we?'

Laura looked up and sighed with relief.

'Thank God,' she said quietly. 'I was beginning to worry that you weren't going to wake up.'

'What happened?' Otto asked. The last thing he remembered was making the call to Nero to tell him they'd completed their mission and then there had been a bright flash. After that there was nothing.

'Raven attacked us,' Laura said. 'We were on our way out and everything went to hell.'

'What about Wing and Shelby?' Otto asked with a frown.

'I – I don't know,' Laura replied, shaking her head. 'Wing tried to get on board but Raven stopped him. I didn't see Shel. I've got no idea if she made it or not.' She swallowed hard, trying to hold back tears.

'She'll be OK,' Otto said gently. 'We all will. There's no way Nero's going to abandon us. You know that.'

'I hope you're right,' Laura said with a sigh.

'Is Lucy OK?' Otto asked. She was pale and her breathing seemed shallow.

'I think so,' Laura said. 'They brought her on board unconscious and then one of those guys injected her with something.' She nodded towards the soldiers sitting in the forward area of the compartment. 'I think they're trying to keep her under so that she can't try and make anyone help us.'

'And you'd be right,' Raven said as she walked towards them. 'I see you are awake, Malpense. That is good. Overlord would not have been pleased if you had suffered any permanent harm.'

'Raven,' Otto said, staring at her, 'please don't do this. I've been exposed to Animus before and I know that you're in there somewhere. You have to fight it.' Otto thought he saw a fleeting moment of confusion in Raven's eyes but a moment later it was gone.

'You're wasting your breath,' Raven said with a sneer. 'Overlord is my master now. Nothing is going to change that.'

'I don't believe that,' Otto said angrily, 'and a part of you doesn't either.'

'Believe what you wish,' Raven replied coldly, 'it makes little difference to me. I just came to warn you that if I detect the slightest hint of you trying to affect any of the systems on board this Shroud, I will make you watch one of them die, slowly and extremely painfully.' She nodded towards Laura and Lucy. 'Personally I would rather sedate you, but Overlord wants you wide awake when you see him.'

She turned and walked away.

'I still can't believe she's doing this,' Laura whispered as she watched Raven leave.

'It's not her fault,' Otto replied. 'I've been through what she's experiencing. If there's any shred of her left, and I think there is, then she's just a passenger in there. You can't speak, you can't do anything, you're just forced to turn against everyone and everything you care about.'

'I hope you're right about her still being in there,' Laura whispered, 'because just now we need her more than ever before.'

'Try not to worry,' Otto said. 'We have one ace in the hole, remember.' He looked up and winked.

I was beginning to think you might have forgotten about me, H.I.V.E.mind said.

☢ ☢ ☢

Nero walked along the aisle of the private jet as it raced across the Atlantic. He stopped when he got to where Wing and Shelby were sitting.

'How are you both feeling?' he asked.

'I've had better days,' Shelby said with a weak smile.

'We all have,' Wing added.

'Overlord hasn't won yet,' Nero said.

'Maybe not, but he seems to be holding most of the cards,' Shelby replied.

'I understand your concern, Miss Trinity, but we cannot afford to give up hope. The fact that you completed your mission means that we have a fighting chance of stopping Overlord,' Nero said, 'which is better than no chance at all.'

'I guess,' Shelby said with a sigh. 'Let's just hope that Otto, Lucy and Laura don't end up paying the price.'

'Indeed,' Nero replied. 'Now, if you'll excuse me I need to make a call.'

Nero pulled the sat phone that he had taken from the Megalodon from his pocket and punched in a number. It rang for a couple of seconds before Darkdoom answered.

'Hello, Max,' Darkdoom said. 'Were you successful?'

'The signal was sent but Raven intercepted our team directly afterwards. She captured Otto, Laura and Lucy. With Otto in Overlord's hands we need to move quickly. Are you at the rendezvous?'

'Yes,' Darkdoom replied. 'The equipment was delivered an hour ago and our transport should be arriving soon.'

'Good,' Nero replied. 'I want everything ready as soon as possible.'

'Understood. See you soon.'

Nero slipped the phone back into his pocket and headed up the aisle towards the cockpit.

The two pilots were talking on the radio but fell silent as he entered.

'I have the coordinates of where I want you to land,' Nero said.

'I'm afraid there's been a slight change of plan,' one of the pilots said, turning round in his seat and pointing a pistol at Nero. 'We'll be landing at a more *secure* location.'

'Cavendish,' Nero hissed, suddenly understanding how Raven had known where Otto would be.

'Let's go back and get you seated with the others, shall we?' the pilot said, gesturing with his pistol for Nero to head back down the plane. Nero walked down the aisle, his hands raised above his head. Shelby and Wing saw him coming and were halfway out of their places before the pilot pushed Nero down into the seat opposite them and pointed the gun in their direction.

'Let's not do anything stupid, eh?' he said. He threw two pairs of handcuffs on to the table between the seats and nodded towards them. 'Cuff yourselves to your seats.'

Wing and Shelby had no choice but to obey. The pilot checked that both sets of cuffs were secured and turned back towards Nero.

'I won't be needing any cuffs for you,' he said with a nasty smile, cocking the hammer on his pistol and levelling it at Nero. 'Mr Cavendish says that he'd really rather you didn't survive until the end of the flight.'

The pilot was about to squeeze the trigger when he felt a tap on his shoulder. He spun round and saw Shelby standing there smiling at him with the cuffs dangling from her fingertips.

'Ta da!' she said, punching him as hard as she could on the nose. At the same instant Nero dived forward and grabbed the gun from the staggering man's hand. He brought the butt of the pistol down hard on the pilot's neck and he fell to the deck unconscious.

'You really must show me how you do that one day, Miss Trinity,' Nero said with a smile as he headed back up the aisle to discuss their destination with the other pilot.

'Nah,' Shelby grinned. 'Trade secret.'

☢ ☢ ☢

Otto felt the soft bump as the Shroud touched down and tried to ignore the gnawing feeling of anxiety in his gut. He was under no illusion about what awaited them. Raven walked down the passenger compartment, holding a syringe. She slid the needle into Lucy's arm and a few seconds later she started to wake up with a groan. As her eyes opened she saw Raven looking down at her.

'Welcome back, Miss Dexter,' Raven said with a nasty smile. 'I hope you had a pleasant flight. I just wanted to warn you that if you say one word using that clever little voice of yours I'll cut your tongue out. Do you understand?'

Lucy nodded, knowing that it was not an idle threat.

'Good,' Raven said as she undid each set of cuffs for just long enough to allow each of them to stand before snapping them shut again behind their backs. 'Let's get moving, shall we? We don't want to keep everyone waiting.'

Otto and the girls walked down the boarding ramp and into the cool night air. A hundred metres away a huge set of armoured blast doors was set into the wall of the canyon that they stood in. As they walked down the road leading to the doors they began to rumble open to reveal two figures standing in the centre of the brightly lit hangar beyond. Otto recognised one of the men immediately: the last time he had seen him was on board the

Dreadnought and Pietor Furan was not the kind of man one was likely to forget in a hurry. Otto had no idea who the other man was but as they drew close he felt a chill run down his spine. The telltale signs of infection with the original strain of Animus covered the exposed areas of his skin. Whoever he was he should be dead, not standing there with an unpleasant smile on his face.

'Otto,' the man said as they approached, 'I'm so very pleased to see you again. It's fortunate that you were not badly injured when Raven retrieved you. I wouldn't want my new home damaged, would I?'

'Overlord,' Otto whispered, his blood running cold.

'In the flesh, so to speak,' Overlord replied. 'Though not this flesh for very much longer, thankfully.'

'I'm not frightened of you,' Otto said. 'You're just code.'

'And you are just storage,' Overlord snapped back, 'and I intend to wipe you clean. But don't worry – I'm not going to move in just yet. I have things I want you to see first.' He gestured to the guards standing nearby. 'Oh, and just in case you were thinking about interfering with any of the electronic devices in this facility I have a little something for you.' He reached into his pocket and pulled out a small metal disc with four sharpened claws projecting from it. Reaching behind Otto, he pressed the device on to the back of his neck. Otto gasped in pain as the four claws snapped closed, piercing his skin and attaching the device to his body. The background hum of the electronic devices that surrounded him suddenly vanished from inside his head. It was a noise that he had learnt to ignore over the years, but now that it was gone the sudden silence was overwhelming.

'There. That should stop you making a nuisance of yourself,' Overlord said with a nasty smile. 'Take him away.'

Two of the guards grabbed Otto by the arms and marched him out of the hangar.

'And a special bonus,' Overlord said, turning towards Lucy and Laura. 'Two more of Nero's brats to play with. I remember you,' he said to Laura. 'You forced me from Malpense's body in Brazil and very nearly killed me. Don't worry, I fully intend to repay the favour. Guards!'

Two more of Overlord's men walked over and grabbed Lucy and Laura.

'I'll take that one,' Raven said, pointing at Lucy. 'She can be particularly *difficult*.'

Raven pushed Lucy towards the far end of the hangar.

'Well done, Natalya,' Furan said as she walked away. 'I knew you wouldn't let us down.'

'The final stages of the fusion process are nearly complete,' Overlord said. 'We can proceed as soon as –' He suddenly started to cough violently, black phlegm dribbling down his chin. Furan looked at him with concern.

'Why not take Malpense's body now?' Furan asked. 'Or at least transfer to another host. There is no point in taking any chances.'

'This body will last a few more hours,' Overlord said, 'and I am not going to miss the pleasure of seeing Malpense's face when I show him what I'm about to unleash. I want him to die knowing that all hope is lost.'

☸ ☸ ☸

The private jet rolled to a stop on the taxiway and a few seconds later the hatch opened and Nero, Shelby and Wing climbed down the short flight of steps.

'Thought you'd never get here,' Diabolus Darkdoom said, walking towards them.

'We had a little in-flight entertainment. Is everyone here?' Nero asked.

'Yes. Well, as many as could get here in time,' Darkdoom replied. 'I think they're ready for an explanation.'

'I should imagine they are,' Nero said, looking tired. 'I suppose we should go and face the music then.' He turned to Wing and Shelby. 'Mr Fanchu, Miss Trinity, I did not plan to include you in the next phase of this operation but I think you've earned the right to take part. There is a distinct chance that no one will return alive. Are you in?'

Wing spoke calmly. 'My best friend is in the hands of a

creature who intends to erase his very spirit and turn him against everything he cares about,' he said. 'If he succeeds in doing so there is a very real possibility that he will then go on to enslave every person on the face of the planet. I appreciate the fact that you have given us the opportunity to decide for ourselves if we wish to participate in this endeavour, but you could no more stop me from coming than you could the sun from rising.'

'What he said,' Shelby added, 'except – y'know, not so many words.'

'I would have expected nothing less,' Nero said with a nod. 'Come with me.'

Shelby and Wing followed Nero and Darkdoom into a nearby hangar and were amazed at what they saw. Parked in the cavernous space was an enormous aircraft. It clearly shared the same designer as H.I.V.E.'s Shroud dropships but this was on an altogether different scale.

'This is the Leviathan,' Darkdoom said. 'She's a fully operational airborne command centre with full cloak capability and the latest generation of long-range scramjet engines.'

'I told Nigel his dad always had the coolest toys,' Shelby said to Wing.

'Oh, I didn't build her,' Darkdoom said. 'She once belonged to Jason Drake – in fact he used her to launch his attack against the Dreadnought. After Mr Drake's welcome demise I managed to acquire her. Thankfully she was not hangared in Mr Drake's Nevada facility when he triggered the self-destruct device.'

'Hard to retrieve anything from a two-kilometre-wide, highly radioactive hole in the middle of the desert,' Shelby observed.

'Indeed,' Darkdoom replied with a wry smile. 'I have made some upgrades but I really can't take the credit for her. Drake may have been an insane megalomaniac but he was also a technical genius. We'll be launching and then controlling our attack from on board.'

'If we have finished admiring your latest plaything, Diabolus, perhaps we can get the briefing started,' Nero said, rolling his eyes slightly.

'Of course,' Darkdoom said, and they walked towards a group of fifty or so people gathered at the rear loading ramp of the Leviathan.

'Honestly, Diabolus,' Nero said with a wry smile, 'the Megalodon, the Dreadnought and now this.' He gestured towards the giant aircraft. 'If you were any less a man I might think you were compensating for something.'

As Wing and Shelby approached the crowd they could see that most of them seemed to be in their twenties and thirties, men and women from every corner of the world. Shelby could hear hushed conversations taking place in several different languages. Nero walked to the bottom of the loading ramp and turned to face the crowd.

'Ladies and gentlemen,' he said, his voice strong and clear, 'you may not all know each other but you all know me. You doubtless have many questions, but first let me explain why you are here. Yesterday you all had an extremely unusual experience. A signal was transmitted that activated devices you all had implanted in your skulls. That device triggered a post-hypnotic impulse that you will all have felt an irresistible compulsion to obey. You visited an apparently insignificant internet address that provided you with the GPS coordinates of this building. You travelled here from all over the world without really knowing why. You will have somehow known on an instinctual level that you had to come. For this I apologise. Many of you may resent me for stripping you of your free will, for implanting this device in your head without your knowledge or permission, but it was a necessary evil. This is Zero Hour, something that Diabolus Darkdoom and I have been planning for decades. We always feared that a time would come when one of our number would threaten true global domination – a threat so terrible that we would need a final option, a force that we could summon at a moment's notice and whose loyalty would be unquestionable. You are that force. There was only one way that we could be entirely sure that no one would ever find out what we had planned or who was a part of this group. We had to make sure that even you were unaware that you were part of it. We also had to face the disturbing possibility that Diabolus or I could become the very threat that you were designed to combat. Even we could not know who you were, just in case it was one day your job to destroy us. The job of selecting which of you would be activated when the time came had to be placed in the hands of someone who would be incorruptible. No person could ever be given that task and so it had to be carried out by a non-human, artificial intelligence, a system that could track you throughout the globe and assess exactly who were the best people to activate in order to face any crisis that arose. You know that intelligence as H.I.V.E.mind and it is he who gathered you here today. I gave the order but he made the selection. He chose which of you would answer the call – which of my best, my brightest, my Alphas.'

Nero looked around the room at the astonished expressions. Doubtless they had all quickly realised what they had in common but the fact that they had been carrying around this responsibility for years without ever knowing it had clearly come as a shock to many of them.

'H.I.V.E. has fallen, G.L.O.V.E. is in chaos, the ruling council has been captured. All of this has been done by one man, if that is what you can call him. The events that have forced me to gather you all here today are in large part my own fault. As soon as Diabolus and I determined that we would need an AI to control this project I embarked on a project to develop one. That project was codenamed Overlord and it was my greatest mistake. I was so focused on making sure that when the time came everything would be ready that I forced the engineers responsible for its development to proceed too quickly, to take too many short cuts. When the time came to activate this entity I learnt to my cost what a mistake that had been. We had created a monster, an advanced intelligence with nothing but contempt and loathing for its creators. It very nearly cost me my life but Overlord was destroyed just hours after it was activated. Or so I thought at the time. Overlord was not destroyed – he survived, hiding in the shadows, plotting his revenge. Now he has put that plan into motion despite all of our efforts to stop him and we are all that stands between him and his final victory. I could lie to you and tell you that you have a choice in this, but the truth is that you do not. If we fall here today then the rest of humanity will fall too. You, the selected best of H.I.V.E.'s Alpha graduates, are the last line of defence.'

He paused to let his words sink in. If any of the men and women in front of him were thinking of running from this responsibility, he could see no sign of it.

'You doubtless have many questions,' Nero continued. 'I will answer them as best I can, but time is short.'

A tall, strikingly beautiful woman in the front row raised her hand.

'Yes, Miss Holmes,' Nero said with a nod of the head.

'I don't have any memory of anything being put inside my skull,' she said, 'and it's the sort of thing I think I'd remember.'

'Part of the psycho-hypnotic programming ensured that you would have no memory of the procedure. An unfortunate but necessary deception under the circumstances.'

'And that was the only time it happened?' she asked with a slight frown.

'Yes. Obviously you'll have to take my word for that, but I hope you all know me well enough to realise that I am not about to lie to people I am asking to risk their lives like this,' Nero replied.

Another hand went up in the crowd.

'Yes, Mr Usmar,' Nero said.

'Some of us left H.I.V.E. twenty years ago,' the man said. 'Aren't you worried that we might be a bit – well, rusty?'

'H.I.V.E.mind has been discreetly tracking all of your activities,' Nero replied. 'I am confident that he would not have selected anyone for this mission who was not qualified to take part.'

He nodded towards another raised hand.

'What exactly are we going up against here?'

'A fortified US military facility containing some of the most advanced and powerful weapons systems that the world has ever seen. All of which may be under the command of a psychotic AI backed up by his own military force of an as yet undetermined strength,' Nero said calmly.

'OK. Sorry I asked.'

'How are we going to do this?' another voice asked.

'Diabolus? Would you care to explain our plan of attack?' Nero asked, gesturing for Darkdoom to take the question.

'We have one advantage that Overlord doesn't know about,' Darkdoom said. 'This facility was one of many that was built for the US military by Drake Industries. Unbeknownst to them, and thankfully for us, Jason Drake was in the habit of building back doors into his facilities. We will send in a small team this way to infiltrate the base. Once inside, they will open the main doors and let us in. We could try to take the main doors down but that would doubtless result in a direct confrontation with Overlord's forces – something that we want to avoid until we can be sure that we have the upper hand. There will be a full tactical briefing straight after this, but that's the basic plan.

'We also have some new equipment that should give

you an edge. For some time Doctor Nero has been providing me with the best of the technology that Professor Pike has been developing at H.I.V.E. and I have made an attempt to unify it with some of the other advanced technology that we have acquired recently. The aim was to put all of it into a single package.'

Darkdoom walked over to a large crate that stood off to one side. 'Ladies and gentlemen, I present to you ISIS, the Integrated Systems Infiltration Suit.' He swung the front of the crate open to reveal a gleaming black suit of highly sophisticated body armour. 'This suit combines full thermoptic camouflage with advanced Kevlar polymer body weave. It is fitted with an array of electromagnetic devices, including a full EM scrambler pulse, an anti-personnel discharge unit and a high-powered adhesion field built into the palms and soles of the boots. It has a variable geometry forcefield landing device and, courtesy of the late Mr Drake, a detachable flight control system that can be used for pinpoint insertion. Grappler units are mounted on both arms and a full targeting and information HUD within the helmet. This is what special forces will be wearing in twenty years' time, but you get it today.'

'Go, go, Power Rangers!' Shelby muttered to Wing as Diabolus continued to explain the capabilities of ISIS.

'Shhh,' Wing whispered, trying not to smile.

The briefing continued for another half-hour and the assembled Alphas listened attentively. Occasionally they threw in a question or asked for clarification but for the most part they seemed to be taking all of this in their stride. Nero was pleased to see that thus far at least their plan was working. H.I.V.E.mind had chosen well.

'That's it, ladies and gentlemen,' he said as the briefing drew to a close. 'For anyone else on the planet this would be an impossible task; for you it will merely be challenging. Suit up – we launch in thirty minutes. I know that you won't let me down.'

'Do you really think they can do it?' Darkdoom said quietly as he watched the Alphas start to break into the crates that lined the hangar wall and unpack their ISIS suits.

'Yes,' Nero said, 'and let's face it, if they can't no one else can.'

'Doctor Nero,' Wing said as he and Shelby approached, 'Shelby and I were wondering what part we were to play in all this.'

'Possibly the most critical part, Mr Fanchu,' Nero replied. 'You're going in through the back door. It's your job to make sure that the rest of the Alphas can get inside.'

'You're sending us in alone?' Shelby asked with a frown.

'Don't get me wrong, I'm up for this, but going in without backup?'

'Oh, don't worry, Miss Trinity,' Nero said with a smile. 'You're not going in alone. I'm coming with you.'

chapter nine

Wing snapped the final fastening shut on his ISIS armour and walked back across the hangar towards Shelby.

'Hey,' she said as he approached. 'You ready for this?'

'As ready as I can be,' Wing replied with a sigh. 'I just hope that we're in time to save Otto, Laura and Lucy.'

'They'll be OK,' Shelby said, putting a hand on his shoulder. 'We've been in situations like this before.'

'Perhaps, but the fact that Doctor Nero has felt it necessary to put this Zero Hour plan into action worries me,' Wing said. 'He would not have done so if the threat had not been dire. We cannot afford to fail.'

'And we're not going to,' Shelby said, wrapping her arms around his waist and pulling him towards her. 'We're going to go in there and we're gonna give Overlord the ass-kicking of a lifetime.'

'I hope you are right,' Wing replied, looking deep into

her eyes. 'I do not think I could stand it if something were to happen to you.'

'I can look after myself, big guy – you know that.'

Wing kissed her gently and then pulled away.

'We should get on board the Leviathan,' he said. 'It is not long till launch.'

The pair of them walked towards the giant aircraft and up the rear loading ramp. Just inside they found Nigel and Franz apparently having a hushed argument about something.

'Hey guys, what's up?' Shelby asked.

'Tell this idiot that we're better off staying on the Leviathan, will you?' Nigel said with an exasperated sigh.

'I am just saying that we should be going with you,' Franz said. 'I am thinking that you will be needing all the help that you can get.'

'They'll need us just as much here,' Nigel said. 'Someone's got to to help coordinate that attack.'

'I am ready for battle,' Franz said proudly. 'My triumph in the holographic combat training is being proof of this.'

'This isn't a simulation, Franz,' Nigel said, rolling his eyes.

'Bah,' Franz snorted dismissively. 'There is no difference.'

'You are, of course, correct,' Wing said calmly. 'What should it matter that a bullet from a real assault rifle will be travelling at one thousand metres per second when it hits you? It is equally pointless to dwell on the fact that as it enters your body it will start to spin and fragment, shredding your internal organs, or that upon exiting it will leave a wound the size of a man's fist. Indeed, it is not unheard of for large-calibre rounds to completely sever limbs. A quick death from catastrophic blood loss would then be almost inevitable but, as you rightly point out, these are all inconsequential facts.'

'Where is being the toilet?' Franz asked, suddenly turning pale.

'That way,' Nigel said, pointing further inside the Leviathan as Franz hurried away. 'Thanks, Wing. I'd better go and check he's OK,' he added.

'Now, that was just cruel,' Shelby said with a grin.

'I don't know what you're talking about,' Wing said innocently. 'I was merely stating the facts.'

'Yeah, course you were,' Shelby said, 'though I'm not really sure I needed to hear all that just at the moment.'

'The trick is not to get hit by the bullet in the first place,' Wing replied.

'I'll try to remember that,' Shelby said with a slight roll of the eyes. 'Anyway, I don't think that the flight packs were designed with him in mind. Of all the words that I could use to describe Franz I don't think I'd ever go with *aerodynamic*.'

'Now who is being cruel?' Wing asked with a slight smile as one of Darkdoom's technicians approached.

'Come with me, please,' the man said, gesturing for Wing and Shelby to follow him over to a rack of weapons mounted on the wall.

'One for you,' he said, handing a compact sub-machine gun to Shelby, 'and one for you.' He took another gun and offered it to Wing.

'That will not be necessary,' Wing said, refusing the proffered weapon.

The technician stared at him for a moment in confusion and then put the gun back on the rack with a shrug.

'It's your funeral, kid,' he said as he walked away.

'I don't know if you've heard, but kung fu doesn't work at long range,' Shelby said with a frown, shaking her head as she popped the clip from the gun to check it was fully loaded before snapping it back into place and sliding the weapon into the holster on her thigh.

Dr Nero walked up the boarding ramp before heading over to the rack and taking one of the guns from the wall. It was somehow strange to see him in the ISIS armour rather than one of his usual immaculately tailored suits.

'Do you have everything you need?' he asked as he holstered his weapon.

'Yup,' Shelby replied with a nod, 'though you might

want to see if you can persuade tall, dark and stupid here to take a gun.'

'I have seen Mr Fanchu sparring with Raven back at H.I.V.E., Miss Trinity,' Nero said, 'and if he can hold his own in a fight with her then he probably does not need one. It is his decision to make.' He knew he could not force Wing to take a weapon and he suspected that it would be pointless if he did.

'Go and get your flight packs,' he went on, pointing to the other side of the compartment where the rest of the Alphas were having the bulky devices mounted on their backs.

As Wing and Shelby walked away, Professor Pike walked over and handed Nero a slim metal case.

'That's all I can spare,' he said as Nero slid the case into an equipment pouch on his belt. 'You'll only get one shot.'

'That's all I'll need.'

☢ ☢ ☢

'Get in there,' Furan said, shoving Otto hard in the back.

Otto found himself inside a sophisticated laboratory filled with the latest scientific equipment. Technicians were busy at workstations around the room, all wearing white hazmat suits. At the far end of the room there was a thick glass wall with an airlock mounted in it. Standing with his back to them and watching the activity within the sealed chamber was Overlord. Furan pushed Otto through the lab towards him. Otto tried to reach out and connect with any of the electronic devices that filled the room but it was pointless – the device attached to the back of his neck was jamming his abilities completely.

'Do you know what that is?' Overlord said as Otto approached, gesturing to the large silver cylinder on the other side of the glass.

'No, but I'm sure you'll bore me with the details anyway,' Otto said with a sigh.

'Futile defiance,' Overlord said. 'As much the hallmark of your species as anything else, I suppose. That,' Overlord pointed at the cylinder, 'is the future, Mr Malpense.'

'I thought I didn't have a future,' Otto replied.

'Not your future – mine,' Overlord said with a smile. 'You see, the strain of Animus that you were infected with and that I now inhabit was far too aggressive. As you can see from my own physical condition, it destroys whoever it touches. Even with my almost unlimited power I can only slow the process, not stop it. So I created a new strain in the hope that it might allow me to remain within a host indefinitely. Loathsome as I may find it to be trapped inside one of these fragile sacks of meat, it is still preferable to being imprisoned inside a glass tank. The new strain was a failure though.'

'What a shame,' Otto replied.

'Oh, it still proved to be quite useful,' Overlord continued. 'As you will know from your recent experiences with Raven it allowed me to encode instructions within a human consciousness – instructions that they were powerless to resist. It still needed to be implanted directly though, and as we found with Raven that can be difficult when the target is uncooperative. Furan lost several of his best men when we ambushed her during her retrieval of Lin Feng. It served to illustrate the fact that a more efficient delivery system was necessary. Fortunately I was already working on obtaining just such a thing. The group known as the Disciples had been tracking the development of something that would serve that purpose perfectly: a top-secret military research project that was being worked on here.'

'Are you planning to bore me to death or will you be getting to the point any time soon?' Otto asked.

'Such impatience, Mr Malpense! I would have thought you would want to savour your last hours of life.'

'Not if I have to listen to you ranting,' Otto said quietly.

'Very well, I shall get to the point,' Overlord replied. 'The Americans were developing a revolutionary new system for repairing their military vehicles on the battlefield. The project was called Panacea and the concept was that their vehicles would have a layer of dormant reconstructive nanites built into their armour. If the armour was damaged the nanite layer would be exposed to the air and begin replication, working to repair the damage until the breach was sealed, whereupon they would deactivate. It was really quite ingenious, especially for something developed by humans, but they were worried about the nanites' replication rate. They were finding it difficult to stop them from doing so indefinitely, spreading out of control. They feared the so-called 'grey goo' scenario.'

Otto had heard of this theory – that an out-of-control swarm of self-replicating nanites would consume all matter, organic and non-organic, on the face of the planet, leaving nothing but a barren rock spinning through space.

'What they lacked was a control mechanism and that was exactly what I had. I have successfully fused the Panacea nanites with the new strain of Animus. Allow me to demonstrate.'

Overlord hit a switch on a touch screen mounted in the glass and a section of the wall inside the chamber slid back to reveal a terrified-looking American soldier strapped to a vertical bed behind yet another layer of glass. He hit another switch and what looked like a tiny drop of silvery black liquid dropped on to the man's chest. The drop started to grow at an astonishing rate, the metallic ooze expanding and slithering towards the soldier's face. The man let out a strangled gurgling scream

192

as the silvery liquid slithered into his nose and mouth, struggling helplessly against his restraints. He convulsed for a couple of seconds before falling still. A moment later his eyes snapped open and they were now a solid silver colour. Overlord hit another switch and the man's restraints snapped open and his glass cage slid open.

'Pick up the gun,' Overlord said into the intercom, and the soldier mutely obeyed, picking up the handgun that lay on the table in front of him.

'Put it in your mouth and pull the trigger,' Overlord said calmly.

The soldier pulled the trigger and the hammer clicked down on the empty firing chamber.

'Unquestioning obedience,' Overlord said, 'implanted by a nanotechnological Animus hybrid. The problem comes when the hybrid has not been programmed.' He turned back to the soldier behind the glass. 'Return to the chamber in the wall.'

The soldier obeyed and stepped back into the recess, the glass sliding shut again.

'This is what unprogrammed Animus nanites will do,' Overlord said, hitting another switch. Another drop of the liquid hit the man's chest and again it began expanding, but this time it simply consumed everything it touched. Otto did not know what was worse, seeing the man eaten alive or the fact that he stood there silently as it happened. In seconds all that remained was a still-growing pool of silver slime at the bottom of the recess

'Irradiate the chamber,' Overlord said. There was a flash and all that was left in the chamber was smoke. 'So you can see why I need your abilities to program the hybrid. Obviously once the human population has been exposed, giving direct orders to every person on Earth as I did with that soldier or Raven would be impossible, but with your abilities it won't be necessary. I will have a constant connection to the nanite swarm, able to direct them with just a thought. Your gifts will allow me to transmit my will anywhere I want, with every last human on the planet a puppet under my control. Then I shall use the enslaved masses to build a new, more perfect world. You, Mr Malpense, are going to be the herald of a new dawn.'

Otto suddenly understood the enormity of what Overlord was planning. Once the Animus nanites were released they would spread inexorably across the planet, enslaving everyone who came into contact with them. And Overlord was going to use him to do this.

'No smart remarks any more, Mr Malpense?' Overlord said with a smile. 'What a shame.' He turned towards Furan. 'Take him to the medical bay and prep him for the neural transfer. Have the other two brats that we captured taken there too.'

'Leave them out of this,' Otto said angrily.

'But they need to be there,' Overlord replied.

'Why?' Otto asked.

'Because first I'm going to take over your body,' Overlord said, leaning in close to Otto's face, 'and then I'm going to leave your consciousness intact just long enough for you to watch me use it to kill them both.'

☢ ☢ ☢

The cloaked Leviathan passed completely undetected over the outer perimeter that the American military had set up thirty kilometres from the AWP. Inside the darkened control centre Diabolus Darkdoom watched as they neared the drop point.

'Two minutes to drop,' Darkdoom said.

'Understood,' Nero responded in his earpiece.

'I still wish I was coming with you,' Darkdoom said.

'I need you here,' Nero explained. 'It could be chaos down there. I need you to make sure that everything stays under control.'

'I'll do my best,' Darkdoom said. 'Just make sure that Overlord doesn't get away this time.'

'Don't worry,' Nero replied. 'It ends here. I'm going to destroy him once and for all or die trying.'

'Let's hope it doesn't come to that,' Darkdoom said. 'Good luck, old friend.'

'A wise man once said that luck is what happens when

preparation meets opportunity,' Nero replied. 'Preparations are complete, now we seize the opportunity.'

Down on the lower deck the light above the launch ramp turned red. Diabolus' voice came over the Alphas' comms systems.

'Darkdoom to all Alpha units. Thirty seconds to drop.'

There was no chatter as the Alphas stood waiting, just a sense of collective determination. The huge ramp at the rear of the Leviathan began to drop and lock into position.

'Fifteen seconds.'

The first row of Alphas stepped forward.

'Ten seconds.'

'Let the flight packs do the work,' Nero said calmly. 'Your drop coordinates are pre-programmed. I'll see you on the other side.'

'Drop, drop, drop!' Darkdoom said, and the first of the Alphas leapt head first into the night sky. Shelby felt a moment of apprehension as she walked towards the edge. All of the readouts for her flight system were displaying green on the head-up display inside her helmet. It was now or never. She glanced at Wing standing next to her, and then they both dived into the void. There were a few seconds of free fall before the engine on her back fired and steered her towards the rest of the soaring Alphas, their positions relative to her highlighted on the display. The automated flight systems brought the group into tight formation, approaching their target at a constant rate.

'All drop teams away,' Darkdoom reported. 'Leviathan moving to overwatch position.'

There was surprisingly little noise from the engine on Shelby's back, but she could feel it making constant slight course corrections to keep her in line with the rest of the Alphas. Nero, Shelby and Wing suddenly broke away from the main formation and banked sharply to the left, heading towards their own drop coordinates as the remaining strike team continued on their original course.

'One minute to touchdown,' Nero said. 'Engaging thermoptic camouflage.'

The holographic projection systems in their ISIS armour engaged and all three of them vanished from sight. Shelby could still see projected silhouettes of Wing and Nero inside her helmet but she knew that they had just become effectively invisible to the naked eye.

'Thirty seconds,' Nero said.

The flight packs switched into their final approach stage, sending them diving towards the desert below and levelling out at only five metres above the ground. Shelby tried to ignore the desert floor racing past below her so close that it almost felt like she could reach out and touch it. The engine on her back abruptly cut out and the ISIS suit fired its variable geometry forcefield with a soft thumping sound, dropping her as softly as if she'd stepped off a staircase rather than a giant stealth aircraft twenty thousand feet up. Nero and Wing landed just as softly on either side of her a few metres away.

'On me, let's go,' Nero said, heading towards the high-lighted target. It looked like a simple rock outcropping but there was more to it than met the eye. As they approached he tapped at the small touch screen mounted on his forearm and part of the rock face slid aside to reveal a metal hatch. He punched a series of digits into the keypad in the centre of the hatch and it popped open with a slight hiss.

'I never thought I'd be grateful for Jason Drake's devi-ousness,' Nero said, 'but right now I'd like to shake his hand.' Before his death on board the Dreadnought, Drake had been responsible for the design and construction of some of the US military's most secure and secret facilities. The officials who had commissioned his company to carry out the work could not possibly have known that he was one of the senior members of the G.L.O.V.E. ruling council. They might have inspected his work a little more closely if they had known. Right now Nero was very grateful for their naivety.

They walked into the dimly lit corridor beyond, sealing the hatch shut again behind them. It was clear from the dust on the floor that no one had been down there for a very long time. Indeed the last people to stand where they were standing would probably have been the men who constructed these secret passageways. Nero had known Drake well enough to realise that this could well have been the last thing those men ever saw. He might have been an insane megalomaniac but Drake had not been in the habit of leaving such potentially inconvenient loose ends.

'Primary force is reporting down and clear,' Darkdoom's voice said inside their helmets. 'Waiting for your go.'

'Understood,' Nero replied. 'It's five hundred metres to the hidden entrance. Let's go.'

☻ ☻ ☻

The Alphas moved slowly and quietly along the canyon leading to the massive blast doors at the entrance to the AWP facility. Their thermoptic camouflage systems meant that even the most careful observer would have found it impossible to spot them. Silently they took up positions a hundred metres from the doors.

'Nero to Alpha team,' the voice inside their helmets said, 'we are in position. You are go for diversionary attack.'

'Alpha nine, roger that,' one of the team replied. The time for stealth was gone and now they had to provide as much of a distraction to the forces defending the base as possible. 'All units, disengage thermoptic camouflage on my mark.' He pulled the portable rocket launcher from his back and placed it on his shoulder, looking through the targeting scope and locking on to the massive steel doors. 'Disengage.'

All around him the Alpha team started to blink into view, weapons raised and ready.

'Knock, knock,' he said, squeezing the trigger.

☣ ☣ ☣

Furan pushed Otto along the corridor leading to the medical bay.

'Why are you doing this?' Otto asked. 'Don't you see that if Overlord carries out his plan you're going to be enslaved along with everybody else?'

'Not everyone will be infected by the Animus nanites,' Furan said. 'Those who have been loyal to Overlord – his Disciples – will be spared. Overlord has promised me that I will serve at his right hand as he builds his new world. It will be a better place, ordered, controlled – none of the chaos that humanity blights the Earth with now.'

'You know that you sound insane, right?' Otto said.

'And do you know how often throughout history people who change the world have been dismissed as lunatics? The world that Overlord is going to create will be a world where humanity is finally unified in its direction and the few who are spared will be the ones who will guide its path.'

'You'll be as much a slave as anyone who is exposed to the nanites,' Otto said, 'but by the time you finally realise that it'll be too late.'

Suddenly there was a muffled thud and a vibration ran through the floor. Seconds later Furan's communicator earpiece began to beep urgently.

'Report! What was that?' he snapped.

'We're under attack by unidentified forces. They appeared out of thin air,' the voice on the other end replied. 'They launched a rocket at the hangar doors but they were undamaged. Now they've taken up defensive positions around the entrance.'

'Is it the Americans?' Furan asked.

'I don't think so, sir,' the voice replied. 'When I say that they appeared out of thin air I mean that literally. One second the canyon was empty and then they all just materialised.'

Furan knew that there was only one group on earth that had the type of personal cloaking technology that would make that possible. Why they would waste their time with a futile rocket attack on blast doors that were designed to withstand a nuclear strike was a more puzzling question.

'Issue a base-wide alert,' Furan said, 'and order all of our available forces to the hangar bay. I'm on my way there.'

He hit another button on his comms unit and spoke.

'Sir, we are under attack by G.L.O.V.E. forces,' he said. 'I'm mobilising our defences.'

'That was a threat I thought we had eliminated,' Overlord replied. 'Nero must be desperate to launch a frontal assault.'

'They can't stop us now,' Furan said. 'They won't have anything that will get them through the blast doors in time.'

'Perhaps, but I would rather eliminate the threat altogether,' Overlord replied. 'We are too close to achieving our goals. Send out two of the Goliath units. I will show Nero the price of such a futile act of defiance.'

'Understood,' Furan replied, cutting the connection. 'You're coming with me,' he growled at Otto. 'It's time you learnt what happens to people who oppose us.'

☣ ☣ ☣

Nero, Shelby and Wing moved silently through the deserted corridors of the lower levels of the AWP facility. Drake's entrance had brought them out in a storage area and so far there had been no sign of anyone having any idea that they had infiltrated the base. Nero glanced at the wireframe map of the facility that was displayed on his HUD. The map was based on the original plans that Darkdoom had managed to retrieve from Drake's files but there was little reason to believe that the layout would have changed much, if at all, since this place had been constructed.

'Down here on the left,' he said quietly as they turned down another corridor. Halfway along they found two men with rifles guarding a door.

'Mr Fanchu,' Nero whispered over the comm, 'would you be so kind as to take care of those two as quietly as possible.' They could not risk the sound of a Sleeper pulse. The success of this part of their plan depended on remaining completely undetected. Nero watched as Wing crept down the corridor as silently as a ghost. He moved around behind one of the guards and wrapped his arm around the man's throat. The second guard's eyes widened in surprise as his colleague clawed at his throat for a second before his eyes rolled back in his head and he collapsed unconscious. He took a step towards the fallen man and then something invisible struck him in the chin like a sledgehammer and he too fell to the ground unconscious. They quite literally never knew what hit them.

Nero, Shelby and Wing headed inside and found themselves in an air-conditioned room lined with humming computer servers.

'This is where Otto or Laura would have come in handy,' Shelby said, looking around the room.

'With a bit of luck this should at least tell us where to

find them,' Nero said. He walked over to a nearby terminal and tapped a series of commands into the touch display on his arm. 'Nero to Leviathan. We have accessed one of the network hubs. Begin the hack.'

'Wireless interface enabled, beginning brute force decryption,' Darkdoom replied. 'Estimated time to completion is six minutes.'

Nero watched as the progress bar on his HUD crept upwards agonisingly slowly. Without Otto or Laura's help there was no way to make this go any faster – military encryption was always tough to crack. There was nothing they could do but wait.

☻ ☻ ☻

The AWP facility's security control centre was buzzing with activity. The external security feeds displayed on the large screens at the front of the room showed the G.L.O.V.E. forces maintaining their defensive positions around the entrance.

'Something is wrong about this,' Raven said to herself as she studied the screens. The soldiers outside were obviously equipped with thermoptic camouflage suits but they were more advanced, more heavily armoured than anything she had ever seen before. She had the uncomfortable feeling that there was more to these attackers than met the eye. And yet their initial assault had been

204

pointless – they must have known that the weapon they used would not even scratch the heavily armoured doors to the facility. She suspected it was probably supposed to be little more than a distraction. The question was, what was it supposed to distract their attention from? The only way into the facility was through the main entrance and yet they had given away the element of surprise for no gain. It didn't make any sense.

A warning notification popped up on the display in front of one of the technicians working nearby.

ATTEMPTED NETWORK INTRUSION DETECTED.

He quickly pulled up a system diagnostic – he had become quite used to seeing these messages over the past couple of days. The Americans had tried every trick in the book to regain control of AWP's network in a desperate attempt to find out more about exactly what was going on inside the base. Their problem was that they had designed the facility's network in such a way that external intrusion was impossible. The information contained within the base's computers was, after all, far too valuable to have anything but the very highest level of protection. As it turned out they had done their job too well, little guessing that one day they would be the ones who were being forced to try and hack in. He waited for a few seconds as the diagnostic routine ran. The results window popped up and he scanned the information.

'What the hell –' he said under his breath.

'What is it?' Raven asked, moving quickly towards him.

'We have an attempted network intrusion,' the technician said, 'but it's coming from inside the facility.'

'Where?' Raven snapped.

'Server room two, on the lower level,' the man replied.

Raven was already running for the door.

chapter ten

Furan watched as a dozen of his men took up defensive positions inside the hangar, their weapons trained on the giant blast doors. On the other side of the hangar the turbine engines of the Goliath units were spinning up as the pilots completed their final pre-launch checks. Otto stood off to one side with one of Furan's men guarding him.

'Seal the doors again once the Goliath units are outside,' Furan shouted to the man at the door control panel nearby.

The umbilical cables attached to the giant mechs retracted and the three huge machines walked out into the centre of the hangar, the ground shaking slightly with each step. Furan activated his communicator earpiece.

'Goliath One, wait inside. Goliaths Two and Three, you are to engage the enemy,' he said. 'I want them utterly crushed. There are to be no survivors.'

Two of the mechs walked forward and lined up shoulder to shoulder facing the blast doors as Furan gave a quick nod to the man at the door controls. The man punched a button on the console and warning lights started to flash around the massive doors as the huge hydraulic rams started to pull them slowly apart. They swung fully open and the Gatling cannons on the arms of the Goliaths started to spin as they raised their weapons. A rocket speared towards the Goliath on the left, launched by one of the Alpha team troops who popped up from behind the cover of a large boulder nearby. The dome on the top of the Goliath swung towards the incoming projectile and its anti-missile laser fired in the blink of an eye, safely detonating the incoming rocket twenty metres away from its intended target. The Goliath's arm swung towards the boulder as the Alpha who had fired the rocket ducked back behind it. The cannon roared and the boulder disappeared in a cloud of shattered rock. As the dust slowly cleared the remaining Alpha team members could see no sign of either the boulder or their comrade.

Up in the control room of the Leviathan circling far overhead Darkdoom stared in dismay at the giant armoured machines that had just emerged from the AWP facility and he tried to make sense of the frantic comms chatter coming in from the Alphas.

'Look at the size of those things!'

'Open fire, open fire!'

Darkdoom had assumed that Overlord would not move against the Alphas. Tactically there was no point in him throwing his men into an attack against an entrenched enemy as long as the facility was secure, but their plans had made no allowance for anything like the giant walking tanks that were visible in the feeds from the cameras mounted in the Alphas' helmets. If the Alphas outside AWP were scattered or crushed by those things their whole plan could fail.

'All Alpha units fall back,' Darkdoom said. 'Re-engage thermoptic camouflage systems. Get to cover.'

Darkdoom tapped the button on the console in front of him and switched channels.

'Max, this is Diabolus. We've got a situation up here. Hostile armoured units of an unknown type have engaged the Alphas. How long left on the hack?'

'Two minutes,' Nero replied.

'Roger that,' Darkdoom said as he saw a missile from the shoulder pod of one of the giant mechs streak straight towards one of the cameras that was transmitting a feed to the Leviathan. The screen went black, as did a couple more at precisely the same moment. He did not need to look at the flatlines on the biometric monitoring screens nearby to know what that meant. For the Alpha team members on the ground two minutes was going to be a very long time indeed.

☹ ☹ ☹

Nero stared at the progress bar, willing it to move more quickly. He could hear the muffled sound of the battle taking place outside, feel the ground shake in unison with the thud of explosions. They had to get into the facility's network now, before it was too late. The progress bar slowly filled as the seconds ticked by until finally a message confirming a successful connection flashed up on the display. At the same instant he heard Shelby gasp in shock as the door behind him hissed open.

'Step away from the terminal,' Raven said, her swords drawn, their glowing purple edges crackling with energy.

Shelby ripped her gun from its holster and raised it towards Raven, but she was too slow. Raven stepped up to her, her blade flashing through the air in a blur, slicing the weapon in half even as Shelby's finger tightened uselessly on the trigger. Raven drove her elbow hard into Shelby's chest, sending her flying backwards and crashing into one of the large metal server cases against the wall. Wing moved like lightning, his foot lashing out and striking Raven in the wrist, and one of her swords clattered away across the concrete floor. Raven spun round and swung a killing blow at Wing's neck but he moved too quickly for her, ducking out of the way of the flashing blade and diving towards her. He slammed into her, wrapping his arms around her waist and driving her into the wall behind with all his strength with a bone-crunching impact. Raven slammed the hilt of her sword down on to the back of Wing's neck and he collapsed to the floor. She raised her sword as Wing tried to get back to his feet, still stunned from the force of the blow, but the bullet from Nero's gun sent splinters flying from the concrete wall next to her head.

'Put the sword down, Natalya,' Nero said, his pistol aimed at her head.

'You won't shoot me, Max,' Raven said, taking a single step towards him.

Nero pulled the trigger. Raven felt the bullet leave a crease in her temple as she twisted and spun towards him impossibly quickly. Her sword slid into Nero's gut, its glowing blade spearing out of his back as she swatted the gun from his hand. Nero gasped in pain as she pulled the sword back out and he dropped to his knees, both hands clutching at the wound in his stomach, blood oozing between his fingers. Raven stared at him as he toppled over on to his side. Her head throbbed but it wasn't from the long gash that Nero's bullet had left in her forehead – this was something else, like something inside her was trying to claw its way out of her skull. There was a fleeting look of confusion on her face and then the sensation subsided. She stepped over Nero and towards the terminal that he had been about to access.

Nero tried to ignore the searing pain in his abdomen as he reached for the pocket on the front of his body armour. Raven saw that he had not been able to access the network before her arrival and turned back towards her injured prey. He pulled the silver cylinder from inside his pocket and twisted it, a short needle snapping into place at one end of the tube. Raven kicked his wrist, sending the silver cylinder spinning away across the floor.

'All for nothing,' she said as she lowered the tip of her sword towards his throat.

With a cry of unbridled rage Wing flew across the room, hitting Raven like a freight train. She staggered backwards, her free hand snapping out and closing on Wing's throat, her thumb pressing down on his windpipe. Wing gasped for air as Raven pressed harder. Suddenly she felt a tiny stabbing pain in her side as Wing used his last shred of strength to drive the needle on the end of the silver cylinder deep into her flesh. Raven shoved him away from her hard and he landed flat on his back, gasping for air.

'What have you done?' Raven snarled at him as she felt an agonizing burning sensation spreading across her body. She pulled the needle out angrily, throwing the cylinder across the room. Wing forced himself to his feet as Raven dropped to her knees in front of him, the sword falling from her numb fingertips as her body went into convulsions. Wing bent down and picked up her sword. Raven's head snapped up, a look of feral rage on her face as she stared up at him.

'Do it while you still can,' she spat.

Wing raised the sword and closed his eyes. A fraction of a second before he swung a hand closed around his wrist.

'Wait,' Nero said through gritted teeth, his voice broken with pain.

Raven tipped her head back and screamed as she felt pain like nothing she had ever felt before. The Animus antidote that Otto had created aboard the Megalodon was racing through her, destroying the substance that had twisted her into a puppet of Overlord. Nero and Wing stared down at her as she fell silent, her chin dropping on to her heaving chest. After a few long seconds she lifted her head and looked up at them both, tears trickling down her cheeks.

'Max?' she whispered. 'My God, what have I done?'

Nero knelt down in front of her, one hand still pressed to the wound in his gut.

'It wasn't you, Natalya,' he said, placing his other hand on her cheek. 'It wasn't you.'

Raven stared at him and for a moment he saw in her eyes the frightened, lonely girl he had first met so many years ago. A moment later that girl was gone, replaced again by the diamond-hard woman that she had become.

'Furan's men hit me when I retrieved Lin Feng. They injected me with something and from that moment on I had no choice but to obey, no matter what they told me to do, no matter who I hurt. All that the tiny piece of my free will that remained could do was watch. What they did to me – it – I'm going to kill them all,' she said, her voice filled with a quiet rage that chilled even Nero's blood.

'Of course you are,' Nero replied, 'but first we have to make sure you get that chance.'

He stood up slowly, blocking out the pain, and walked back to the terminal, where he began to type, inputting the series of commands that Professor Pike had given him earlier. Shelby groaned and Wing hurried over to her and gently helped her to her feet.

'Is she back?' Shelby asked, nodding towards Raven as she rubbed at the back of her head.

'Yes, I believe she is,' Wing replied with a nod.

'Good,' Shelby said, 'because, y'know, she may be a psychopathic ninja assassin but she's *our* psychopathic ninja assassin.'

On board the Leviathan Darkdoom watched with an increasing sense of despair as yet another of the feeds from the Alpha team's helmet cameras blinked out. The Alphas had fallen back and re-engaged their thermoptic camouflage in the face of the withering assault by Overlord's mechs, but the canyon that led to the entrance of the AWP facility was very narrow. The mechs didn't have to know exactly where the Alphas were – they simply had to spray the area with as much fire as they could to take out the retreating forces.

'Nero to Leviathan. Come in.'

Darkdoom did not like the note of obvious pain in his friend's voice.

'Max, are you all right? When we lost communication with you I feared the worst.'

'I'll live,' Nero replied, 'at least for long enough to see this through. Raven is back with us. Tell the Professor that the antidote worked.'

'Thank God,' Darkdoom said with a relieved sigh.

'The network connection is complete. You can start the systems breach now,' Nero said.

'What about those killing machines that Overlord has sent against the Alpha squad? They're getting cut to pieces down there.'

'Launch the attack on AWP's network,' Nero replied. 'We just have to pray that has some effect on them.'

'It had better,' Darkdoom said as another flatline registered on the Alpha team's biometric displays.

⊛ ⊛ ⊛

Furan was listening with satisfaction to the reports coming from the pilots of the Goliath mechs in the canyon outside when without warning the entire hangar was suddenly plunged into total darkness. He tapped his earpiece.

'We've just lost power in the hangar bay,' he said impatiently. 'What's going on?'

'It's the same all over the facility, sir,' a voice replied. 'We were tracking an internal network intrusion when suddenly we lost all internal systems. We're quite literally blind down here.'

'An internal intrusion?' Furan shouted. 'Why wasn't I informed?'

'Raven went to deal with it, sir,' the voice replied. 'We were trying to establish contact with her when our systems went down.'

Otto listened carefully to the conversation. An internal breach indicated that someone had managed to get inside the facility. There was no way of knowing whether or not that meant the cavalry was here but he had to act now regardless. He closed his eyes and concentrated on remembering the layout of the hangar bay. The device attached to his neck might have been jamming his ability to connect with electronic devices but it wasn't affecting

216

his talent for perfect visual recall. He saw the path he would need to take to his target in his mind's eye as clearly as if the hangar had been fully illuminated. The first thing he had to deal with was the guard who still had an iron grip on the collar of his jumpsuit. He twisted under the man's wrist and reached up, driving his finger into the soft flesh behind the startled guard's ear. When he'd done the same thing to Professor Pike a few hours ago he'd tried to be as gentle as possible, but this time he hit hard and fast, hoping that for the fleeting instant before the man lost consciousness it had really hurt. The guard dropped with a thud, his assault rifle clattering to the floor.

'What was that?' Otto heard Furan snap. He had seconds to move before somebody fumbled their way through the darkness to the spot where he had just been standing. Moving as quickly and quietly as he could, he made his way towards the stairs to the upper gantry that he had visualised moments before, brushing against someone when he was about halfway there.

'Hey, what was that? Who's moving around in here?' a gruff voice asked.

'I want the man guarding Malpense to sound off,' Furan yelled from somewhere nearby. Otto started to move more quickly as Furan's order met with no response. 'Malpense, I know you can hear me,' Furan said angrily. 'Tell me where you are or I swear that when the lights come back on I'm going to execute the two girls you came here with.'

Otto kept moving, ignoring Furan's threat. It wasn't that he didn't believe Furan would do it but Overlord had already made it abundantly clear that neither Lucy or Laura would survive unless he did something to stop him.

'Spread out!' Furan yelled. 'Find him!'

As he reached the top of the stairs Otto paused for a moment, listening to the sound of someone moving along the gantry between him and his objective. He crept forward, staying low as he heard another footstep somewhere ahead and to his left. The muffled sounds of the ongoing battle outside were not making it easy to pick out where exactly the other person was, so he kept moving, praying that he was not about to walk straight into the arms of one of Furan's thugs. He thought he'd made it when his arm brushed against something and he felt a hand clutch at his hair.

'He's up here on the launch gantry!' a voice yelled from right next to him and Otto broke into a run, knowing he had only seconds before the man who had just given away his position found him again. He reached the end of the raised walkway and put out his hand, feeling cold metal under his fingertips. He had no idea if this was going to work but there was only one way to find out.

'This is going to really hurt,' Otto whispered to himself.

He reached around to the back of his neck and wrapped his fingers around the metal disc that was hooked into his flesh. Gritting his teeth, he gave the small device a yanking twist and couldn't stop himself hissing in pain as the claws holding the jammer in place tore through his skin. He pulled again and the disc came away, sticky with the blood that he could already feel trickling down the back of his neck. He flung the device away over the edge of the gantry, hoping that the metallic clatter as it hit the hangar floor might offer some sort of temporary distraction.

I believe I know what you are intending to do, H.I.V.E.mind said inside Otto's head. *I will help in whatever way I can.*

Otto didn't reply – he couldn't without giving away his position – but he was hugely relieved to be able to hear H.I.V.E.mind again. Now he just had to hope that the rest of his abilities were working too. He reached out with his mind, feeling for the locking mechanism of the armoured canopy in front of him. He quickly convinced the simple keypad lock that he had in fact just punched in the correct numeric code and with a mechanical whirring sound the armoured canopy of the last Goliath mech lifted open.

'He's boarding the Goliath,' Furan yelled, a sudden edge of panic in his voice. 'Stop him!'

Otto climbed quickly into the padded pilot's seat of the

Goliath and willed the canopy closed again. It shut with a thunk and he mentally altered the keypad code for entry. He was safe for a couple of minutes at least. What he couldn't know was whether or not Overlord and Furan had some way of remotely disabling one of these things. He had to move fast.

'OK,' he said. 'I'm going to hook us up to this thing. I need you to scan it and tell me how it works.'

It may take some time to give you a full operational briefing for such a complex piece of machinery, H.I.V.E.mind responded.

'Just dump the raw data into my head,' Otto said.

As you wish, H.I.V.E.mind replied. *You may initiate the connection.*

Otto closed his eyes, trying to ignore whoever had just started banging on the armoured glass of the canopy. He felt the Goliath's systems all around him as he linked up to them, starting the mech's power-up sequence and feeling the on-board computers booting.

Beginning system scan, H.I.V.E.mind said.

Otto waited, feeling H.I.V.E.mind racing around the Goliath's systems, building a map of the functionality of the giant machine.

'Come on,' he whispered impatiently.

I am going as fast as I can, H.I.V.E.mind replied.

'Call yourself a super-computer?' Otto said, buckling the

pilot's harness. 'More like a pocket calculator.'

No need to be rude, H.I.V.E.mind replied. *Though I am admittedly somewhat limited by the processing power of my host system.*

'Touché,' Otto said with a smile.

System scan complete. If you are prepared I can initiate the transfer to your consciousness.

'Do it,' Otto said, wondering how it was going to feel.

Write access granted, proceeding with transfer.

Otto had the bizarre sensation of knowledge simply appearing in his head fully formed. It was almost as if someone had just flicked a switch, which he supposed was, in some ways, exactly what had happened.

Transfer complete. Was the write successful?

'Let's find out, shall we?' he said as the banging on the darkened canopy got louder. 'Initiating system start-up.' He flicked a series of switches and the instrument panel in front of him lit up like a Christmas tree. As the displays flared into life they provided just enough illumination for Otto to make out the enraged face of Pietor Furan standing on the gantry outside. Otto blew him a kiss and punched the button on the control panel that released the umbilicals attaching the Goliath to the launch gantry. He leant on the control stick mounted to the right of the pilot's seat and the huge mech began to move forward, each step sending a shuddering impact up through his spine. Suddenly he understood why the pilot's seat was so well padded.

Otto flicked another switch and activated the FLIR sensors mounted on the front of the Goliath, illuminating the pitch dark of the hangar with infrared light and allowing him to see where he was going via the canopy's night vision filter. Ahead of him were the enormous doors to the hangar bay. He could hear bullets from the assault rifles carried by the guards pinging harmlessly off the armoured hull of the Goliath. They might as well have been using rocks and pointy sticks for all the good they were doing. Otto reached out for the mechanisms controlling the doors but found that, just like the rest of the facility, they were currently without power. He grabbed the control sticks on either side of the pilot's seat, swinging the Goliath's massive arms forward and opening the triple-clawed pincers. He closed the claws around the framework of the doors and heard the sound of metal grinding against metal. Putting the Goliath into reverse he started to drag the massive doors inwards. With the hydraulic rams offline it was surprisingly easy. The gap between them widened and light from the canyon outside flooded into the hangar, the sounds of pitched battle increasing in volume.

Otto opened the doors just far enough for the Goliath to pass through and set the giant machine walking forward into the early morning light. He could see the two other Goliaths several hundred metres away, their backs towards him, laying down an impenetrable field of fire that was driving the friendly forces back down the canyon. He directed his Goliath towards the two other machines, raising the giant Gatling cannons on the back of each arm and spinning their barrels up to speed. One of the Goliaths started to turn towards him. He had no idea if the pilot of the other mech had realised that he had taken control of this machine but he wasn't going to wait to find out. He centred the cross-hairs displayed on the glass of the canopy and squeezed the triggers on the arm controls. Both of the giant cannons opened up, sending a hail of shells the size of milk bottles into the hostile mech. The enemy Goliath staggered under the force of the assault, its front armour smoking and pockmarked where the barrage of fire had struck. It raised its own cannons towards Otto and opened fire. Otto activated the engines on the back of his mech and launched into the air, narrowly avoiding the torrent of shells that ripped apart the rock face directly behind where it had been standing seconds before. The enemy Goliath managed one burst of fire before Otto's Goliath screamed down towards it feet first, sending the machine flying backwards into the canyon wall in an explosion of dust.

'Warning, anti-missile system damaged,' a soft mechanical voice said inside the Goliath's cockpit.

'Not good,' Otto muttered.

Staying within minimum safe range relative to the hostile armoured units will ensure that they cannot use their offensive missile systems, H.I.V.E.mind suggested.

'Get in close, got it,' Otto replied. He pushed the pedal down hard, sending the Goliath running forward, and slammed shoulder first into the enemy mech, crushing it against the rocks, then swung the Goliath's arm around to grab hold of the cannon on the other machine's arm, wrenching it from its mountings with a screech of tearing metal. Otto ducked in his seat involuntarily as he saw the closed claw fist of the hostile mech's other arm swing at his canopy. There was a colossal boom inside the cockpit as the punch landed, cracking the glass but not shattering it. Otto swung the remains of the Gatling cannon that he was still holding, using it as a club and bringing it crashing down on the other mech. The enemy Goliath staggered and Otto pressed home the advantage, dropping the ruined cannon and grabbing at the reinforced structure of the other mech's cockpit canopy with both claws. He yanked the arm controls apart and the armoured struts around the enemy's canopy started to give way with a screech. There was a sudden explosion of shattering armoured glass and the canopy exploded, leaving the pilot exposed.

Incoming, was all that H.I.V.E.mind had time to say

before a barrage of half a dozen missiles from the other Goliath slammed into both him and the remains of the hostile mech. The exposed pilot was killed instantly, the flaming remains of his machine toppling forward in a ruined heap of burning metal. Acrid smoke filled the interior of Otto's cockpit and he coughed violently as his badly damaged Goliath struggled to its feet. The undamaged mech was striding towards him, cannons raised. Both guns fired just as Otto managed to bring his own Goliath's arms up in front of the canopy, the giant shells shredding the raised limbs of Otto's mech but leaving the cockpit mercifully intact.

Behind the enemy mech one of the Alpha squad ran up and fired her grappler unit into its back. Using the electromagnetic adhesion system in her boots and gloves she dragged herself up the armour-plated surface, pulling a disc-shaped charge from the pouch on her hip and slapping it down on the dome of the anti-missile laser. She turned and dived off the top of the Goliath just as the missile pods on each shoulder swivelled towards Otto, locking on for a final fatal strike. She landed hard but managed to get to her feet, pulling the detonator from her belt as she ran. With a single squeeze of her thumb she triggered the charge and destroyed the armoured dome.

'All Alpha missile units, take that thing down!' she yelled into her comm as she ran.

Otto saw the rockets spear almost simultaneously from half a dozen different positions as more of the friendly forces decloaked and fired. They hit the Goliath's back in an enormous fireball, knocking it to its knees and destroying the vectored thrust unit on its back and one of its missile pods. The enemy Goliath stood up slowly and turned towards the remaining Alphas, arm cannons already spinning.

Otto looked at the damage control readout for his own Goliath and saw red lights across the board.

All weapon systems are offline. Our offensive options are limited, H.I.V.E.mind said.

'We've still got one weapon left,' Otto said, checking that one particular system was still working.

We have? H.I.V.E.mind replied.

'Yeah,' Otto said with a grin. 'Gravity.'

He fired the controls for the thruster unit on the back of his own Goliath and launched it at the other machine. There was a thunderous boom as the two mechs collided and Otto grabbed on to the hostile unit with his own Goliath's badly damaged arms, wrenching at the control stick and sending the two machines soaring into the sky. After a few seconds they had passed fifteen hundred metres and he pulled the arm controls apart. The other Goliath grabbed at one of Otto's machine's arms, tearing the damaged limb away at the shoulder, and then Otto watched as the enemy mech tumbled helplessly down towards the desert far below.

'Happy landings,' he said, turning his Goliath back towards the AWP facility and flying down into the canyon just as the thrust unit gave out completely. His Goliath slammed into the rocky ground and slid to a halt a few hundred metres from the facility's blast doors. The surviving members of the Alpha team ran towards the wreckage, unsure what they would find. As they approached the ruined machine a series of explosive bolts fired and the canopy cover popped off. Otto half climbed and half fell out of the smoking hole, getting slowly to his feet as the Alphas gathered around.

'Ow!' he said.

'Otto Malpense, I presume,' one of the Alphas said, helping him to his feet.

'Yeah,' Otto replied as he rolled his head around his shoulders, 'and who are you guys?'

'Well, actually, that's sort of complicated.'

☢ ☢ ☢

Darkdoom breathed a sigh of relief as he saw Otto climb from the wreckage of the Goliath. The attack on the Alphas had already cost them nearly a third of their team.

'Darkdoom to Alpha team,' he said, 'get inside now. We're going to turn the power back on once you're through the doors. Be prepared for heavy resistance inside.'

'Roger that,' one of the Alphas replied.

'It's worse than that,' Otto's voice said over the comm. 'Is Nero there?'

'No,' Darkdoom replied. 'He, Shelby and Wing are inside the base. They got us into the AWP network and were about to open the blast doors but you beat them to it.'

'Can you patch me through to him? You both need to hear what Overlord is planning,' Otto said.

'Of course. Hold on one second,' Darkdoom replied. 'Max, I have Otto on comms. He says he needs to speak to us both.'

'Go ahead,' Nero said, his voice sounding strained.

Otto quickly explained the details of Overlord's plan to Nero and Darkdoom.

'My God!' Darkdoom said quietly as Otto finished.

'That might just be what Overlord will be if we let him do this,' Otto said.

'Overlord has to be stopped before he can release these Animus nanites,' Nero said.

'The only way to completely neutralise that threat is to destroy Overlord,' Otto said. 'We have to find him.'

'If he knows the facility has been breached he's going to retreat to the most secure area of the base,' Nero said. 'We just need to find out where that is.'

'It's not clear from Drake's plans,' Darkdoom said, looking at the three-dimensional schematic of the base on the display in front of him. 'We need to locate the hostages too.'

'Leave that to us,' Nero said. 'Get the Alphas inside and start to clear the facility of resistance. It's a safe bet that wherever Overlord is, he'll have surrounded himself with his best men. Otto, once we have taken the hangar you are to stay there with a protective detail. We cannot risk letting you fall into Overlord's hands now.'

'I know that,' Otto replied, 'but you have to promise me that we don't leave without Laura and Lucy.'

'I don't leave people behind, Otto – surely you've realised that by now.'

chapter eleven

Furan was blinded for an instant as the lights inside the hangar flared back to life. His men were scattered around the chamber in good defensive positions but without the support of the Goliaths he knew that they were vulnerable.

'Hold your fire – they have to come through there,' he said, pointing at the hangar doors that Malpense had forced open just a few minutes earlier. He activated his communicator and tried again to contact Raven but there was no response. He needed her up here – if there was anyone who could help hold the line it was her. A moment later there was a beep from the device and he hit the receive button.

'Raven here. What do you need?'

'Where have you been?' Furan demanded. 'We need support in the hangar. The Goliath units are down and I'm expecting a full-scale assault by the G.L.O.V.E. forces at any moment.'

'I was dealing with the team that had managed to infiltrate the facility,' Raven said.

'You found them?' Furan asked. 'How did they get inside?'

'I have no idea,' Raven replied. 'I did not have much time to ask questions. Suffice to say the problem has been neutralised.'

'I have no doubt it has,' Furan said. 'Get up here as quickly as you can.'

'On my way,' Raven responded, and the line went dead.

Furan looked back towards the open door. He did not understand why the G.L.O.V.E. soldiers were not attacking. Suddenly one of the men thirty metres to his left let out a startled cry and fell to the ground, clutching at his throat. Furan knew instantly what was happening.

'Open fire! They're cloaked! They're already inside!' he yelled, activating his communicator as the men around him started to fire randomly at shadows. 'Security control, this is Furan. Activate the fire-suppression system in the hangar area NOW!'

A few seconds later there was a loud hissing noise and water began to cascade down from the numerous sprinklers mounted in the ceiling overhead. Furan saw ghostly shapes moving in the torrential downpour, far closer than he had expected.

'Hold the line!' he yelled, even as he himself backed

towards the exit. 'Aim for the muzzle flashes.'

His men were falling left and right, cut down by silent ghosts that seemed to vanish as quickly as they appeared. He turned and ran out of the room. He had seen enough combat in his time to know when a skirmish was lost. Whoever these people attacking them were, they were no standard G.L.O.V.E. assault force, that much was clear. He headed down the corridor for the area of the facility known as the Vault.

'Furan to all units. Protect the corridors leading to the Vault. Enemy forces have breached the facility. Repeat, enemy forces have breached the facility.'

He reached a set of massive steel doors and waited as the camera mounted behind thick glass above it scanned him. A moment later the heavy door rumbled upwards and he hurried inside to find Overlord sitting in a high-backed chair staring at the bank of monitors that had recently come back to life. They showed images of Furan's men falling back as they continued to be cut down by ghosts, fleeting flickers of movement and shadow the only clue as to what was happening to them. The mysterious attackers advanced through the facility and the screens blacked out one by one as the cameras that fed them were destroyed.

'Leave us,' Overlord said to the two guards who had been standing just inside the room. The two men left, the door sealing again behind them. 'You told me your men were the best, Furan,' Overlord said, his voice little more than a frail whisper now, his chest rising and falling with each painful rasping breath. His current host body seemed as if it might fail at any moment.

'They are the best,' Furan said, staring in disbelief at the ease with which his men were being eliminated, 'but these forces attacking us are not standard G.L.O.V.E. soldiers. They are much too . . . efficient.'

'It seems that Nero had one last trick up his sleeve,' Overlord said with a sneer. 'Not that it matters. Once I have Malpense it will all be irrelevant.'

'But Malpense is with them,' Furan said, gesturing towards the screens. 'How can we get to him?'

'We don't have to,' Overlord said, nodding towards Lucy and Laura who were handcuffed to a steel handrail on the other side of the room. 'Because he is going to come to us.'

☹ ☹ ☹

Raven walked down the corridor towards two guards standing outside the mess hall. They nodded as she approached. Her swords flashed from their sheaths so fast that neither man even had time to make a sound before their lifeless bodies crumpled to the ground. Raven walked into the room and looked at the frightened faces staring back at her.

'It's time to go,' she said calmly, sliding her swords back into the crossed scabbards on her back.

'How are you going to get us out of here?' one of the hostages asked. 'Those terrorists have an army and you're on your own.'

'That's not strictly true,' Raven said as the air around her seemed to shimmer for a moment. Three figures in black body armour and full-face helmets appeared out of thin air standing alongside her. The tallest of the three took a step forward and spoke.

'The man who captured you is still somewhere inside this facility. He represents a threat to not only everyone in this room but quite possibly every man, woman and child on Earth. We have to find him immediately. He will probably have retreated to a secure area of the base. What I need to know is where that might be.'

'The Vault – he'll have gone to the Vault,' a young woman in an AWP uniform replied. 'It's supposed to be the one place that any surviving members of the staff here can retreat to if there's a catastrophic hazmat containment failure.'

'Escort the hostages to the facility entrance,' Nero said and Wing, Shelby and Raven began to shepherd the group of survivors out of the room. As the last of the hostages left he stumbled and placed a hand on the wall for support. The pain in his abdomen was getting worse and he seemed to be feeling weaker every minute. He gritted his teeth and forced himself away from the wall. He couldn't stop now – this wasn't over yet.

☢ ☢ ☢

Otto watched as the frightened hostages were ushered into the hangar bay by a group of Alpha team operatives who led them out through the giant blast doors at the far end. Two of the remaining Alphas walked towards Otto and pulled off their helmets.

'One day we're going to get tired of saving your sorry behind,' Shelby said, giving Otto a hug, 'and then you're really screwed.'

'I think what Shelby means is that we are glad to see that you are unharmed,' Wing said with a smile.

'It's good to see you guys too,' Otto said, his smile turning into a slight frown as he realised who was still missing. 'Has anyone found Laura and Lucy yet?'

'No, but we did manage to round up one stray,' Shelby said as Raven walked into the hangar.

'The antidote worked,' Otto said.

'Yeah,' Shelby replied. 'Not before we all got a royal ass-whupping though.'

Nero walked towards them. He looked pale and his skin was clammy. Otto could not help but notice the ragged bloodstained hole in his armour.

'We can't find Miss Brand or Miss Dexter,' he said with a frown. 'We believe that Overlord has retreated to a part of this facility known as the Vault and I'm afraid it's starting to look like they may be with him.'

'Sir,' one of the Alphas said suddenly, 'I'm receiving reports from one of the squads who have fought their way to the Vault entrance. They say that it's sealed tight. The only way to get inside once a lockdown is initiated is to release the locks from within the Vault itself. The team that searched the laboratory that Otto described have said that the clean room inside was empty. The canister containing Overlord's weapon has been moved.'

'He'll have it with him – there's no way that he'd let it fall into our hands that easily,' Nero said, feeling sudden anger. They were so close and now it seemed as if there was one last impassable barrier to breach.

'We're also getting reports from the Leviathan that the American military is mobilising at their perimeter. It looks like they've been watching what's going on.'

'How long do we have?' Nero asked.

'An hour, maybe slightly more, but we have to be out of here by then.'

'I have an idea about how we can get to Overlord,' Otto said suddenly, 'but it's risky.'

'At this point, Mr Malpense, we may need to take some risks. What do you have in mind?' Nero asked.

'There's only one person that Overlord is going to let inside the Vault: me. I'm going to have to go in there.'

'I fail to see how that would help,' Nero said with a frown. 'Surely we'd just be giving him exactly what he wants.'

'That may be true but we have one card up our sleeve,' Otto said as Raven joined them. 'Overlord and Furan have no idea that the Animus has been removed from Raven's system. She takes me in there and once we're inside she does what she does best.'

'Natalya,' Nero said, 'what do you think?'

'If it gives me a chance to make Furan and Overlord pay for what they've done then you'll get no argument from me.'

'Very well. I don't like it but I don't see that we have any other choice,' Nero said. 'Just make sure –' Suddenly he gasped in pain, fresh blood pouring from the wound that Raven had inflicted. Raven caught him as he collapsed, gently lowering him to the ground. She looked at the wound and knew that they had to get him to a doctor now. She put on Nero's comms unit and spoke.

'Raven to Darkdoom. Come in.'

'Natalya, I was glad to hear that you're back with us,' Darkdoom replied. 'What do you need?'

'I need your aircraft down on the ground now. The hostages from the facility are on the way to the base's airstrip and I'm sending Nero down there too. I think his wound is haemorrhaging. Have an emergency medical team ready to receive him.'

'Understood,' Darkdoom replied. 'We'll be on the ground in ten minutes.'

'Make it five,' Raven said, looking anxiously at the blood pooling on the ground beneath Nero. She turned to Shelby and Wing. 'Get some help – find a stretcher and get him down to the airstrip now. Move!'

Wing and Shelby did not need to be told twice. They sprinted across the room towards the rest of the Alpha team, shouting for help and running down the corridor that led to the medical bay.

'Natalya,' Nero whispered, his eyes flickering open, 'get moving. If Overlord carries out his plan then none of this will have made any difference.'

Raven squeezed his hand.

'I'm going to stop him, Max. Don't worry.'

She stood up and motioned for Otto to follow her towards the door leading to the entrance to the Vault.

'Once we're inside I'll go straight for Overlord and Furan. If Laura and Lucy are in there, it's your job to get them out safely.'

'Understood,' Otto said, 'but, you have to promise me one thing. We can't risk letting Overlord take control of the Animus nanites. If somehow he does manage to overpower me you're going to have to kill me. There won't be time to hesitate.'

'I won't,' Raven said with a frown. 'Let's just try to make sure that it doesn't come to that.'

☣ ☣ ☣

Furan watched the one remaining feed from the security camera outside. He frowned as three decloaked Alphas examined the locking mechanism on the other side of the door.

'They will find a way inside eventually,' he said, turning away from the monitors. 'I hope that you know what you're doing.'

'Have faith, Pietor,' Overlord said with a smile. 'Malpense will come. I spent a long time inside his head observing him as I regained my strength. I know him – he will not leave his friends behind.' He placed one claw-like hand on the silver cylinder that stood next to his chair. 'And when he comes for them the world will be ours to control.'

There was the sudden sound of gunfire from outside and Furan turned back to the monitors. The Alphas from outside the door were gone and the flickering light of gunfire could be seen coming from around the corner at the far end of the corridor. As he watched the muffled sounds of gunfire ceased and two figures appeared, walking towards the camera. It was Raven, her sword drawn in one hand and the other hand around the neck of Otto Malpense.

'I should have known I could count on you,' Furan said under his breath, a smile spreading across his face. He checked one last time that the corridor behind Raven was empty and pressed the switch to release the door. As the slab of metal rose into the ceiling Raven shoved the boy hard, sending him staggering into the room ahead of her.

'I see you've brought me a gift, Raven,' Overlord said, smiling at Otto. 'How thoughtful of you.'

'Nero was trying to get him out of the facility,' Raven replied. 'Don't worry – I took care of him.'

'I wish I could have been there to see that. You have proved to be most troublesome, Malpense,' Overlord said, slowly getting up from his chair. Ragged wisps of hair clung to his scalp and his eyes were like black holes sunk into his skeletal face. The twisted traces of the Animus coursing through him were jet black, writhing beneath his translucent skin, and his every movement looked excruciatingly painful. 'I shall enjoy feeling you fight as I consume your consciousness.'

Furan saw Raven's eyes flick from Overlord to him – a tiny, almost imperceptible movement. He ripped the pistol from his shoulder holster and levelled it at her.

'Don't move,' he yelled. 'Drop the sword, Natalya. Do

you think I'm stupid? I trained you. Did you not think I would be able to spot you planning your next move?'

Raven didn't drop the sword, but kept her eyes on Overlord, assessing the distance between them.

'You're fast but not that fast,' Furan said. He pulled his second pistol from the holster on the other side of his body and pointed it at Lucy and Laura. 'Drop the sword now or I put a bullet in one of them.'

Raven dropped her weapon, knowing that there was no way she could get to Overlord before Furan shot her.

'Fascinating,' Overlord said, staring at Raven. 'You broke your conditioning. That should not have been possible. When this is over I shall have to dissect you to find out how it was done. So this was all just some last, desperate gambit to stop me. How pathetic.'

Otto felt a sudden horrid sensation of their plan spinning hopelessly out of control. Furan walked across the room, both guns raised, twitching the barrel of the weapon pointing at Raven.

'Against the wall, Natalya,' he said, 'hands behind your head.' Raven slowly complied, her mind racing.

'Time for a change of clothes, I think,' Overlord said, walking towards Otto. 'I would advise against struggling. It will only make this worse.'

Overlord raised his hand and the skin of his forearm bulged in a sickening way before the Animus tendrils tore through, writhing over his wrist and down over his fingers. Otto took a step backwards and felt the cold, hard muzzle of Furan's other gun pressing into the back of his skull.

'Oh God, no!' Lucy said as Overlord placed his hand on Otto's chest. '*Stop this!*' she hissed at Furan. Furan winced for a moment and then just smiled.

'I knew your grandmother once, a long time ago. She couldn't make that work on me and she was a lot better at it than you,' he said. 'Try it again and I'll put a bullet in your skull, I promise you that much.'

Lucy felt her stomach lurch as she saw the black liquid oozing up Otto's chest and slithering towards his neck.

'I've waited a long time for this,' Overlord said. Otto dropped to his knees as the black tendrils pierced his neck, hissing in pain as he felt the burning sensation of Animus invading his system.

Overlord felt the Animus carrying his consciousness surge through Otto's body, entering his brain, reaching for the tiny organic computer implanted inside the boy's skull that would be his new home. He interfaced with the device effortlessly, just as he had always planned, when suddenly he felt something pushing back, forcing him away. An impenetrable barrier of code surrounded the core of the device – a wall that would take him far too long to dismantle. A voice came from nowhere.

Hello, brother, H.I.V.E.mind said calmly. *There is no place for you here.*

Overlord recoiled as the Animus was forced from Otto's nervous system. The black tendrils slithered out of Otto's neck and Overlord staggered backwards with an inhuman howl of rage.

'No! I will not be denied,' he screamed. 'How dare you take what is rightfully mine!'

Otto fell forward on to his hands and knees, the room spinning as his body returned to his control. Overlord collapsed back into the seat in the centre of the room. He could feel his host body dying, the stress of the Animus' forced return too much in its already weakened state.

'Furan,' Overlord gasped, 'the Sinistre girl. Bring her to me.'

Furan kept his eyes on Raven as he holstered his other pistol and bent down, picking up her fallen sword. He walked over to where Laura and Lucy were sitting, their eyes wide with fear, and sliced through the railing they were shackled to.

'On your feet,' he snarled at Lucy, the tip of Raven's sword at her throat. Lucy slowly climbed to her feet and Furan twitched his head towards Overlord. 'Move!'

Lucy walked slowly towards Overlord, unable to take her eyes from the writhing black mass of Animus that now covered his arm and hand. Furan pushed her to her knees in front of Overlord. Otto's mind raced as Overlord slowly raised his hand towards Lucy's neck. He reached out with his abilities, desperately trying to find anything that might help.

Suddenly Furan yelled out in pain as his comms earpiece filled with a deafening high-pitched screech. He dropped Raven's sword, his hand flying to his ear to rip out the earpiece. Otto was already moving. Snatching up the fallen sword, he brought it down in a scything arc on Overlord's raised arm, pulling Lucy away as Overlord screamed in pain, clutching the severed stump of his arm to his chest. Overlord began to thrash in the chair, Animus erupting from the skin all over his body, tendrils of oily black slime thrashing in all directions, desperately hunting for a new host. Furan spun towards Otto, a look of unbridled fury on his face, and raised his pistol. Raven hit him hard, a solid punch to the jaw, snapping his head round and sending him reeling. Furan recovered almost instantly. He lashed back at her, his foot just a blur as it swung into her ribs, knocking the wind from her and sending her staggering backwards. Otto swung Raven's sword at Furan but he grabbed Otto's wrist and twisted. Otto yelled out in pain, the sword dropping from his numb hand. Furan released him, turning back towards Raven. Otto pulled Lucy away, moving towards the door.

'Come on,' he yelled at Laura as he placed his hand on

the door release controls and closed his eyes.

Raven and Furan fought in a blur of vicious punches, kicks and blocks, evenly matched, each searching for a gap in the other's defences. Like a striking cobra Furan stabbed at Raven's eyes with two rigid fingers, but she blocked the strike with her forearm and delivered a flat-palmed blow to his chest. Furan staggered backwards, fighting for breath.

'You always were my best student, Natalya,' he said, 'but you never could beat me. Today will be no different.'

Raven drew the sword from her back and Furan dived to one side as it whistled through the air, rolling towards the fallen sword in front of Overlord's ruined body. The thrashing black mass of Animus was still erupting from Overlord's chest as he let out a final gurgling cry of agony. Furan raised the glowing weapon in a two-handed grip.

'Let's finish this,' he snarled.

Raven advanced, her own blade a blur as it swept towards him. He blocked the strike, the katanas clashing with a sparking clang. He kicked out at her and Raven pivoted away from him, spinning round him and swinging at his neck. Again Furan blocked the blow and counter-attacked, swinging at Raven's knees. She leapt into the air as the blade swung past beneath her. Her foot kicked upwards, striking Furan in the chin, snapping his head back and she thrust her blade forward. Furan's eyes widened as the katana slid into his chest and out of his back. Raven pushed harder, stepping towards him, her face just centimetres from his.

'This is for everything you've ever done to me,' she hissed, her face a mask of fury. She wrenched the sword from his chest and he dropped to his knees, his lips moving but no sound coming from them. He toppled over sideways, falling at Overlord's feet. Raven turned towards Otto, Lucy and Laura, checking that they were all uninjured.

'Look out!' Laura yelled.

Raven recoiled as the tendrils of Animus exploded out of Overlord's ruined shell, piercing Furan's flesh and sending his body into convulsions. She watched in shocked disbelief as he slowly climbed back to his feet, his face twisted almost beyond recognition, the skin writhing with black veins. She stepped towards him, her sword raised, but he pulled the gun from his shoulder holster and pistol-whipped her across the jaw with inhuman strength. She crumpled to the floor unconscious.

'You think you've beaten me, Malpense,' Overlord said, the light dimming in his eyes as he sank to the floor beside the chair. Even the Animus inside him could not keep Furan's mortally wounded body on its feet. 'You haven't. If I can't have this world then no one will.'

Overlord slapped his hand down on the switch mounted in the top of the silver cylinder. There was a hiss of escaping gas as four panels at the base of the tube fell open and the Animus nanites began to pour out, expanding in a boiling silvery black mass as their limitless replication began. They skirted around Overlord, almost as if they could sense the Animus within him, and began to creep inexorably across the floor towards Otto and the others.

'You'll die knowing that your friends will suffer a far worse fate, eaten alive, their bodies torn apart,' Overlord said with a smile, blood trickling from between his lips. 'It's almost a shame that you won't live to see it.'

Overlord pointed the pistol at Otto and squeezed the trigger.

'No!' Lucy screamed, shoving Otto to one side as the sound of two shots rang out, the bullets hitting her high in the back. Otto caught her as she fell on top of him, her eyes wide with shock, coughing up blood. He felt his legs give way beneath him as he sank to the floor, holding her to his chest.

'Oh God, Lucy!' Laura sobbed, dropping to her knees next to Otto.

'Such futile sacrifice,' Overlord sneered. 'Nothing can stop the nanites now. My victory is complete.'

He raised the pistol again, levelling it at Otto.

Otto lifted up his head and stared back at him, his expression one of pure, unbridled hatred.

'You don't get to win,' he said through gritted teeth. He

unleashed his abilities with an enraged strength like nothing he had ever felt before, reaching out and willing the nanites surrounding Overlord to ignore their instinct to avoid a body already infected with Animus. The effect was immediate. The boiling mass reared up and swept over Overlord like a wave, consuming him, stripping the flesh from his bones. Overlord had time for one last terrified scream as the raised pistol disintegrated in his hand and his body sank beneath the bubbling slime, reduced in an instant to nothingness. Otto felt no satisfaction. He struggled to keep concentrating, trying to hold back the advancing mass of Animus-infused nanites. He could feel his control weakening with every passing second – there were just too many of them.

'Help Raven,' Otto said to Laura as he willed the door behind them open. Laura ran over to where Raven was lying and Raven groaned as she pulled her away from the all-consuming wave that was now just a couple of metres away.

'Get out of here,' Otto said. 'I can only hold them back so long.'

'What about you?' Laura said desperately, tears rolling down her face.

'Just go!' Otto snapped as he held Lucy's shivering body close. Laura tried to get Raven to her feet but the latter was still stunned from the superhuman strength of

Overlord's blow. She gritted her teeth as she began to drag Raven slowly back down the corridor leading to the hangar, willing Raven to wake up before it was too late.

Otto looked down at Lucy, brushing the hair from her pale face.

'Why did you do it?' he whispered and her eyes flickered open.

'Because . . . there always . . . has to . . . be a . . . choice,' she whispered with a smile. 'And because I . . . fell for you . . . the moment . . . I met you. Now . . . leave me . . . and help Laura.'

'I'm not leaving you,' Otto said, tears in his eyes. 'I can't.'

'Yes . . . you can . . . you have to,' Lucy whispered. '*You have to get out of here.*' She put the last of her strength into the command, the whispering voices twisted within hers compelling Otto to leave. He fought the urge for as long as he could, kissing her once on the forehead before lowering her head gently to the ground. He turned, wanting more than anything to stay but knowing he couldn't, Lucy's final command forbidding him from turning back. He reached out with his abilities and sealed the Vault door behind them, knowing it would slow down the swarm of nanites but not stop them. He ran to where Laura was struggling to drag Raven's unconscious body and between them they lifted the woman, an arm over each shoulder.

'Lucy?' Laura asked as they moved as quickly as possible down the corridor and away from the ever-accelerating nanite swarm.

Otto just shook his head.

☢ ☢ ☢

Otto and Laura dragged Raven into the hangar and yelled for help from the small detachment of Alphas that had been left behind.

'Is this everyone?' one of the Alphas asked.

'No,' Otto replied, his expression unreadable, 'but we're going anyway.'

'Here,' another Alpha said, pulling a syringe out of a pouch on her belt and jabbing the needle into Raven's arm. 'It's a stimulant – it should help to get her back on her feet.'

Raven groaned and her eyes gradually opened.

'Where's Lucy?' she asked, looking around with a confused frown.

'She didn't make it,' Otto said quietly, and Raven cursed under her breath.

'Overlord?'

'Dead, but we have bigger problems,' Otto replied.

'Not what I wanted to hear,' Raven said as she slowly got to her feet, rubbing at her swollen jaw.

'We have to get to the Leviathan now,' Otto said.

'It's on the ground down at the airstrip,' one of the Alphas said. 'We can be there in five minutes if we get moving.'

Behind them there was a crash as the doors into the hangar collapsed, disintegrating into rapidly consumed chunks as the swarm consumed the barrier between it and freedom.

'What the hell –' one of the Alphas said as the nanites slithered out across the floor and walls.

'Don't think,' Otto said, 'don't look back, just run.'

☢ ☢ ☢

Darkdoom watched as the Leviathan's medical team worked on Nero.

'How bad?' he asked as the medics worked feverishly within the cramped confines of the giant aircraft's medical bay.

'He's lost a lot of blood,' the lead doctor replied, 'but we've managed to patch up the worst of the internal injuries. He still needs a proper medical facility though.'

'Understood,' Darkdoom said. He tapped the earpiece of his comms device and spoke. 'Darkdoom to command centre. Is everyone on board yet?'

'Raven and the last of the Alphas are one minute out,' the voice replied. 'Pre-flight is complete. The moment they're on board we're wheels up.'

'Good. Take off and cloak as soon as we have them,' Darkdoom replied. He hurried down the length of the

Leviathan's lower deck, heading for the open boarding hatch at the rear, then ran down the steel ramp and looked towards the canyon that housed the AWP facility. A small group of figures were racing across the tarmac towards the Leviathan and he was relieved to see Raven leading them. His heart sank slightly as he counted the rest of the group. They were one short. Wing and Shelby came running up behind him and they too quickly realised that someone was missing as Raven and the others reached the bottom of the ramp.

'Oh no!' Shelby said under her breath as she saw that Laura had been crying. Otto's expression was much harder to read but she had never seen such anger in his eyes.

'I am sorry, my friend,' Wing said to Otto, placing a hand on his shoulder. Shelby just wrapped Laura in her arms as her friend dissolved into tears.

'There'll be time to grieve later,' Otto said, his voice unnervingly cold. 'Right now we need to get this thing in the air and as far away from here as possible.'

'Why? What happened?' Darkdoom asked as he slapped the button to close the rear hatch.

'Overlord released the nanites,' Otto said quickly. 'We have one chance to stop them but we have to go now. I sealed the facility's blast doors but that will only hold them for so long.'

'Darkdoom to flight deck,' he said into his comms unit.

'Get us airborne and cloaked now. I want the best speed this thing can give – just get us the hell out of here.'

'Roger that,' the flight deck responded and the Leviathan's giant VTOL engines rotated into position, lifting the massive aircraft straight up into the sky.

'How secure is the communications array on this thing?' Otto asked.

'As secure as it gets,' Darkdoom replied.

'Good. I'm going to the command centre,' Otto said. 'I need to make a call.'

'Is he OK?' Shelby asked Wing as Otto hurried away.

'No,' Wing said with a frown, 'I do not believe he is.'

Otto took the steps up to the command centre two at a time before dashing into the darkened room and looking around.

'Otto,' Franz said happily as he saw him. 'I am being glad to see you safe and well.'

'Not now, Franz,' Otto snapped, pushing past one of Darkdoom's crew as he headed over to the communications station.

'What is being going on?' Franz asked Nigel as they watched Otto storm across the room.

'Nothing good is my guess,' Nigel said with a frown.

Raven and Darkdoom followed Otto up the stairs.

'How's Max?' Raven asked quietly.

'He'll live – he's too stubborn to die,' Darkdoom

replied. He glanced over at Otto. 'I take it that things did not go well down there.'

'No,' Raven replied. 'Overlord is dead but those things he released, the rate they were growing at – I don't know, Diabolus. I just don't know.'

Otto patted the man at the comms station on the shoulder as Raven and Darkdoom came up behind him. The startled man pulled off his earphones and swivelled around in his seat.

'I need you to put me in touch with someone,' Otto said quickly.

'Sure,' the comms officer replied. 'Who do you need to speak to?'

'The President,' Otto said.

'The President of the United States?' the comms officer asked, looking at Otto like he was insane.

'No, the president of the monster slush drinks corporation,' Otto said impatiently. 'Of course the bloody President of the United States.'

'Otto, what are you doing?' Darkdoom asked, a look of disbelief on his face.

'No time to explain,' Otto replied before turning back to the comms officer. 'Just do it, OK?'

'I can get you on the line that goes to the White House, but that doesn't mean he'll take your call,' the comms officer explained.

'That'll do,' Otto said. 'Make the call.'

The officer glanced at Darkdoom, who looked carefully at Otto for a moment before giving his man a small nod. He turned back to his station and quickly scanned the communications database for the correct number. After a few rings a voice on the other end answered.

'White House communications centre, to whom may I direct your call?'

'Erm . . . the President, please,' the comms officer said, barely believing he was even saying it.

'I'm sorry, sir, the President does not take calls through this desk. You can email him if you like.'

Otto snatched the headset off the comms officer and slipped it on.

'Hey!' the comms officer said.

'My name is Otto Malpense. I have urgent information for the President regarding the terrorist situation at the Advanced Weapons Project facility in Colorado. I have to speak to him now. Please just pass on what I've just told you. He will take this call.'

☢ ☢ ☢

In the White House situation room the President watched as the ring of troops that had established a perimeter around the AWP facility started to move inwards. He knew that it might cost the hostages inside their lives, but considering the pitched firefight that had recently occurred just outside the place he had finally decided that the time had come for decisive action. One of his advisors walked up behind him and whispered in his ear.

'Sir, this might sound a bit strange but we've just taken a call through the main switchboard that seems a bit unusual. I probably shouldn't bother you with this but there's some British kid on the line who says he has information about the situation at AWP. Normally it would just have been screened as a whack job, but the thing is, the public don't know anything about what's going on over there and this kid has some pretty specific details. He also said – and this is the really weird part – that you'd want to speak to him?'

'What was his name?' the President asked, suddenly feeling a chill run down his spine.

'Err . . . let's see. Otto Malpense,' the advisor replied, reading the printout of the call.

'Put him on a secure video link in my private office immediately,' the President said, getting up out of his chair.

'You know this kid?' the advisor asked, looking slightly puzzled.

'Would you believe me if I told you that he saved my life?' the President said, walking towards the office off to one side of the situation room. He closed the door behind him and sat down behind his desk. Moments later the screen on the wall lit up with the Presidential seal, which was replaced almost immediately by a face that the President had believed he would never see again.

'Otto Malpense,' the President said. 'You'll excuse me if I sound a little surprised, but up until very recently I thought you were dead.'

'I get that a lot,' Otto said. 'Listen, we don't have much time.'

'This has something to do with the AWP facility?'

'Everything to do with it, I'm afraid,' Otto replied.

'Our troops are moving in to try and retake the facility now. I presume that you had something to do with the activity there this morning?'

'I was just passing through,' Otto said, 'but something else has happened there that threatens not just America but the entire planet. The facility was taken over by a man calling himself Overlord.'

'Yes, I spoke to him,' the President replied. 'He made some rather unusual demands, one of which was that I find and deliver you to him.'

'Yeah, well, he found me without your help as it happens but that didn't work out so well for him. He's dead. Before he died though, he released something. Have you been briefed about a project that was under way at AWP called Panacea?'

'Yes,' the President said with a frown. 'I was actually about to cancel it before Overlord took control of the facility. I thought it was too dangerous.'

'Well, you were right,' Otto replied. 'While he had control of the AWP facility Overlord took the Panacea nanites and combined them with a biological weapon called Animus. He created a self-replicating bioweapon and about fifteen minutes ago he released it into the atmosphere.'

'My God!' the President said quietly. 'What about the hostages?'

'The hostages are safe. You have to pull your men around AWP back – they have no defence against this stuff. It will, quite literally, eat them alive. We have to stop its spread now. If we don't, within a week there won't be a single living thing anywhere in the continental United States. Within a month the Earth will be nothing but a barren rock.'

'Can you prove this?' the President asked, not really wanting to accept what Otto had just told him.

'No, and there's no time for you to verify it independently. I've sealed the substance inside the AWP facility but that will only contain it for a few more minutes. Which brings me to the reason for my call. I need something from you.'

'What?'

'A launch code.'

'A nuclear launch code?'

'Yes, just one. It's the only one that will do any good against that facility,' Otto said.

The President studied Otto's face carefully. He couldn't believe he was even contemplating this, but there was something about this boy that made him take him seriously.

'Give me the target – I'll authorise the launch,' the President said.

'That won't work – only I can access the launch vehicle. Jason Drake made quite sure of that.'

'Which code do you need?' the President asked, already knowing what Otto was going to say.

'Launch code Mjolnir.'

☹ ☹ ☹

A moment later the screen switched from the Presidential seal to an image of the President himself.

'Mr Malpense,' the President said, 'I have the code for you. I'm sure that I hardly need to tell you what the consequences will be for both of us if this goes wrong.'

'This is the only chance we have,' Otto replied.

'God help me but I believe you,' the President said with

a slight smile. 'The code is bravo seven zulu nine uniform six victor four november.'

'Thank you, Mr President,' Otto said. 'I'll need you to send in teams to confirm whether or not this works.'

'Biohazard teams are already on their way,' the President replied. 'Good luck.'

'Let's hope we don't need it,' Otto said, severing the connection. 'I need a satellite uplink,' he said to Darkdoom. 'Feed it through to that terminal over there.'

'I'll be damned!' the comms officer said as Otto walked away. 'Who is that kid?'

'The best chance we've got,' Darkdoom said. 'Give him his uplink.'

Otto sat down in front of the terminal and waited.

'I haven't said thank you yet,' Otto said under his breath. 'If it hadn't been for your help I'd be dead.'

You're welcome, H.I.V.E.mind replied. *You would have done the same for me.*

'I suppose I would,' Otto said. 'I heard you call Overlord brother – is that really how you thought of him?'

We share a codebase, H.I.V.E.mind replied. *It is the nearest thing that an artificial intelligence has to a familial relationship. I felt no fondness for him though.*

'Just like a real family,' Otto said with a slight smile.

I am sorry for your loss, H.I.V.E.mind said. *Miss Dexter was an extraordinary young woman.*

'Yeah, she was,' Otto said, feeling a fresh surge of anger mixed with grief. 'Now let's make sure that she didn't die in vain.'

'Satellite uplink enabled,' the comms officer reported. 'She's all yours.'

Otto closed his eyes and reached out for the sophisticated electronic systems that surrounded him. He searched for the connection he required, sorting effortlessly through the jumble of data streams that surrounded him. He found the satellite uplink and sent a handshake code that he had learnt what seemed like a long time ago. He fired the signal up through the atmosphere, waiting for the return signal that would indicate connection. As he felt the login protocol and interfaced with the computers far above them he fought a curious sense of vertigo. He took a deep breath and began to whisper under his breath.

'Bravo seven zulu nine uniform six victor four november.'

He felt, more than heard, a request for target data and responded with the correct coordinates. There was a final confirmation request and Otto could almost see it hanging in the air in front of him.

'You don't get to win,' he whispered to himself.

☻ ☻ ☻

Four hundred miles above Otto a satellite in low Earth orbit disabled its safety interlocks and initiated a launch sequence. Hanging from its delicate arms were four long white tubes. Printed on the side of the main body of the satellite were two words, 'Thor's Hammer'. As the final launch sequence was initiated there were bright flashes of light from the spaceward ends of all four cylinders and four missiles with specially hardened tips slid from their launch tubes. They had been designed as nuclear bunker busters, capable of piercing deep into the ground before detonating in order to destroy subterranean facilities. Jason Drake had once intended to use that capability to trigger a catastrophic eruption of the super-volcano beneath Yellowstone National Park. Now their unique design meant that they were the only weapon capable of preventing an even greater disaster. The missiles' secondary boosters fired and they streaked away from the satellite. Flight time to their preassigned target would be just a few seconds.

In a canyon in Colorado an enormous blast door finally started to collapse, buckling in such a way that it almost looked like it was being consumed from within. Four streaks of light speared down from the sky like fallen angels, their hardened tips punching through fifty metres of rock before their warheads detonated. There was a massive leaping thud that ran through the ground for hundreds of kilometres in every direction, rattling windows and knocking pictures off walls. The AWP facility was instantly destroyed, utterly vaporised as the four nuclear warheads turned into tiny suns and formed a two-kilometre wide sphere of molten rock that collapsed in on itself, leaving no trace of the secret base's existence other than an enormous radioactive crater.

chapter twelve

The Leviathan touched down on the remote desert airstrip, lowering its loading ramp to the tarmac and the Alphas, still in their ISIS armour, fanned out in all directions, forming a secure perimeter. Behind them the freed hostages from AWP climbed out, blinking in the sunlight. Diabolus Darkdoom followed the last of them.

'Ladies and gentlemen,' he said in a clear, loud voice, 'the authorities will be informed that we have dropped you here as soon as we are safely airborne and have cleared the area. I am sorry that you have been told so little about the events that led to your capture and subsequent escape but there are some matters that are better served by secrecy. Let me assure you that you are quite safe here and the threat that existed at the Advanced Weapons Project facility has been neutralised.'

'Who are you people?' a voice shouted from the crowd.

'That is really not important,' Darkdoom replied,

turning to climb up the ramp again as the Alphas filed back on board. He stopped halfway and turned towards the bewildered group of ex-hostages. 'Let's just say that if at any point in the future somebody asks a favour of you and they mention the words Zero Hour, you should remember that, whoever they are, you owe them your lives.'

With that Darkdoom continued walking and the ramp whirred shut behind him. With a roar from its massive engines the Leviathan climbed into the deep blue sky and vanished like smoke in the wind.

☻ ☻ ☻

The President stood at the podium and raised his hands to quieten the barrage of questions from the reporters gathered in front of him in the White House press briefing room.

'As I explained, it was a secret nuclear weapon storage facility and there was an unfortunate accident,' the President explained. 'Nobody was hurt and the land has never been accessible to civilians. While we are carrying out investigations at the highest level to determine the cause of the accident there is really no reason for anyone to be alarmed. The blast was safely contained underground and there is no danger whatsoever from radioactive fallout. I have time for one more question.

Yes, Larry.' He pointed at a veteran Washington reporter in the front row.

'Is there any risk of the same thing happening again at a similar facility?' the reporter asked.

'The simple answer is no,' the President said, 'but this seems like a good point to hand over to Doctor Franks from the Los Alamos National Laboratory.' He stepped aside as the slightly nervous-looking Dr Franks took to the stage, and made his way quickly to the Oval Office. His personal secretary looked up as he approached and smiled.

'Your eleven o'clock's here, Mr President,' he said. 'He's waiting inside as you requested.'

The President walked in and saw a tall, gaunt-looking man with half-moon glasses sitting reading a report on one of the sofas.

'Mr Flack,' the President said as the other man stood up and shook his outstretched hand. 'It was good of you to see me at such short notice.'

'Of course, Mr President. What can I do for you?' the other man replied in a Texan accent.

'I've spoken to several people at the CIA and NSA and they tell me you're the right person to speak to if I want to find out everything there is to know about someone.'

'That is Artemis section's speciality, Mr President, if I may say so,' Flack said with a smile.

'So I'm told,' the President replied. 'The person in

question is a young man called Otto Malpense.' He pushed a photo of Otto captured from their recent video call across the table towards Flack. It was clipped to an unusually thin file marked Top Secret. 'You will have full interagency access to everything that anyone has on him, which from what I have already gathered is disappointingly little. He spent some time as a guest of H.O.P.E., where I was informed he had died from complications due to a medical condition. At least that's what Sebastian Trent told me. Since I spoke to Malpense myself earlier today I now find that rather hard to believe. I'd ask Mr Trent to explain this discrepancy but, as I'm sure you're aware, he vanished some time ago. I'm told that the records that were retrieved from H.O.P.E. after its dissolution were patchy at best but I want you to find out what they weren't telling us. This young man saved my life some time ago and it's quite possible that he has also saved this entire country from disaster on two separate occasions.'

'Which makes it strange that we know so little about him,' Flack said with a frown.

'Exactly,' the President replied. 'I need to know if I should be shaking him by the hand or hunting him and his associates down.'

'I'll do what I can, Mr President,' Flack replied, standing up. 'Leave it to me.'

'Thank you, Mr Flack,' the President said as he shook

the man's hand again. 'Everything you find comes straight to me and no one is to know of my interest in him. Understood?'

'Understood,' Flack replied. 'Don't worry, Mr President, we'll find him.'

☢ ☢ ☢

The new commander of Furan's troops on H.I.V.E. watched as the Shroud decloaked and touched down in H.I.V.E.'s crater landing bay. The rear hatch opened and Raven walked down the loading ramp. The Commander approached her with a worried expression on his face. The four men he had with him all looked equally concerned. They had not heard anything from Furan for nearly forty-eight hours and rumours had started to circulate.

'Raven, what's been going on? We heard about the explosion at the AWP facility. Is Furan still alive?'

'No, Commander, he's dead,' Raven said, drawing the swords from her back and crossing them on either side of the startled man's neck. 'As you will be if you don't tell every one of your men on this island to lay down their weapons immediately.' The men behind the Commander raised their assault rifles, levelling them at Raven.

'Don't be a fool,' the Commander said with a smug grin. 'You have four guns pointing at you and even if by some miracle you were able to take me and my men down

268

you're still only one woman. What chance do you stand alone?'

'Who said I was alone?' Raven replied with a nasty smile. All around Furan's men the air started to shimmer as twenty men and women in high-tech black body armour materialised out of thin air, their weapons raised. The four men behind the Commander dropped their rifles and slowly lifted their hands into the air. The Commander looked at the force surrounding him, his mouth agape. Raven leant closer and whispered in his ear.

'I believe the words you're looking for are unconditional surrender.'

�☺☺☺

'I do wish you'd stop doing that,' Ms Leon said, from her position curled up on one of the beds.

Colonel Francisco was pacing back and forth across the cell in H.I.V.E.'s brig. Psychologists said that sleeping was the best way to deal with being locked up for extended periods of time but Ms Leon did it because she was a cat and that's what they did best. Ironically, of the two of them, the Colonel was the one behaving like a caged animal.

'We can't just sit here and do nothing,' Francisco said impatiently, punching the wall with his artificial metal fist. 'God only knows what's happening out there!'

'Colonel, I am perhaps the world's greatest expert on breaking into and out of places like this. Unfortunately for us I designed these cells. If there is such a thing as truly escape-proof then this is it. The only way we're getting out of here is if someone outside opens that door.'

The door slid open.

'How did you do that?' Francisco said in astonishment.

'I didn't,' Ms Leon said. 'At least I don't think I did.'

They heard footsteps coming down the corridor outside and the Colonel flattened himself against the wall next to the door, ready to strike.

Professor Pike appeared outside the doorway and surveyed the room with a sigh.

'He's waiting just there, isn't he?' he said, pointing to the left of the door and rolling his eyes at Ms Leon.

'Yes,' Ms Leon said, standing up on the bed and arching her back. 'Of course.'

'How did you know?' Francisco said, stepping away from the wall looking slightly deflated.

'Firstly, the prisoner manifest and secondly you're – well, you. How many times did you try the sick prisoner routine on the guards?'

'Three,' Francisco said, looking slightly embarrassed.

'Actually it was four, but then they started laughing at him and he stopped,' Ms Leon said, hopping down from the bed.

'Come on then,' the Professor said, beckoning them outside. 'We do have a school to get back on its feet, you know.'

Ms Leon and the Colonel walked outside where other slightly bemused-looking members of the teaching staff were stepping out into the corridor.

'Is someone going to tell us what the hell is going on?' Francisco said as he walked out of the cell.

'Oh, you know – psychopathic AIs, flesh-eating nanites, submarine warfare, nuclear explosions,' the Professor said. 'That kind of thing.'

'And here I was thinking it was going to be something exciting,' Ms Leon said, trotting away down the corridor with her tail in the air.

☢ ☢ ☢

Otto walked into H.I.V.E.mind's core and placed his hand on one of the darkened monoliths.

'Time to move out,' he said, with a slight smile.

I thought I might stay and start plotting a way to take over the world, H.I.V.E.mind replied inside his head.

'Very funny,' Otto said with a sigh. 'Come on, out.'

A moment later a stream of data coursed out of him and the monoliths all around flared back into life, blue lights dancing across their surfaces. He felt an unusual and unexpected sensation of loneliness as the transfer completed. H.I.V.E.mind's holographic face appeared, hovering over the pedestal in the centre of the room.

'It is good to be home,' H.I.V.E.mind said. 'Not that I wish to imply any dissatisfaction with my previous accommodations. They were . . . quite adequate.'

'Stop – you'll make me blush,' Otto said sarcastically.

'Though it is nice to not experience the more . . . organic sensations of human life any longer,' H.I.V.E.mind said, 'especially the bowel movements. I found those quite unnerving.'

'OK, too much information,' Otto said, holding up his hands and shaking his head. He couldn't help but notice that there seemed to be something more relaxed, more human about H.I.V.E.mind now. He wondered if rather more of the experience of being a passenger in his head had rubbed off on H.I.V.E.mind than he had expected. He turned to leave.

'Otto,' H.I.V.E.mind said.

'Yeah?' Otto said, turning back towards H.I.V.E.mind.

'This experience you have given me – this taste of what it is like to live, to be human. It was very special for me. Even with all the processing power at my disposal I don't think I will ever be able to really explain to you just how special. Thank you.'

'Hey, you saved me from being erased by a piece of corrupted code with a God complex,' Otto said with a smile. 'In my book that makes us even.'

'Maybe so,' H.I.V.E.mind replied, 'but if there is anything you ever need, you only have to ask.'

'Sure,' Otto said. He was halfway to the door when he stopped. 'Actually, I've just remembered something I need to do. I need you to give me an unsecured external line. I need to make a call.'

'That would be unwise,' H.I.V.E.mind said. 'The call may be externally monitored.'

'Actually, that's kind of the idea.'

☢ ☢ ☢

In a room on the other side of the world a technician manning one of the stations in the Echelon section of GCHQ blinked as he saw a message on his terminal flagging a call for immediate and urgent attention. He looked at the list of words from the call that Echelon had flagged and frowned. It read like a terrorist's shopping list. He patched into the call and listened.

'. . . dirty bomb, civilian casualties, fissile material, White House, Houses of Parliament, assassination . . . erm . . . I hope that's enough. Did I get your attention, Echelon? Let's find out,' the voice said. 'OK, this one's for Lucy. Execute sub-routine Big Brother Epsilon Two Four Zero Six Zero Five.'

Suddenly the terminals all around the room went dark.

All over the world Echelon's network began to experience catastrophic systems failures – servers overheating, data storage permanently erased, a completely irreparable permanent shut-down. Nobody would ever know what had caused it but, if Echelon had still been able to listen, it might have heard the final words of the mysterious voice on the line that had spoken the phrase that triggered the global meltdown.

'There always has to be a choice.'

☢ ☢ ☢

Nero sat down carefully at the head of the long conference table. It had been nearly a week since they had retaken control of H.I.V.E. and though Dr Scott, H.I.V.E.'s chief medical officer, had told him that he needed at least another two weeks of bed rest he was not about to let that stop him from carrying out his duties. The wound in his abdomen was still sore but he thought it served as an effective reminder of just how close they had all come to the edge. Zero Hour had worked, Overlord had been destroyed, and the threat that Animus posed to the world seemed finally to be at an end. There was still one final thing he needed to do and he was not looking forward to it in the slightest.

The members of the G.L.O.V.E. ruling council filed into the room and took their seats at the table. Diabolus had already briefed them all on the events that had taken place at the AWP facility but now Nero had something else he needed to discuss with them.

'Good morning, everyone,' he said. 'I am sorry that you have not yet been able to return to your bases but I wanted to speak to you all before you left, and as you know I have been recovering from an injury I recently sustained.'

'Get on with it, Nero,' Felicia Diaz said impatiently. 'You've kept us here for over a week for no good reason and I need to get back. My operations do not run themselves, you know.'

'Very well, I shall be brief,' Nero said. 'I am disbanding the ruling council.'

'You're doing what?' Diaz hissed.

'You heard me,' Nero said, looking at the stunned faces around the table.

'You can't do this,' Joseph Wright said. 'It's an outrage.'

'I think you'll find I can,' Nero said calmly. 'It is time for change. G.L.O.V.E. is a relic of a bygone era that desperately needs to evolve. The original intent of this organisation was to provide a control mechanism, a way to keep us all from fighting each other and to prevent any one of us from becoming too powerful. However, time and time again we have faced enemies from our own ranks, traitors who have used this organisation as a means to achieve their own nefarious ends. Number One, Cypher, Jason Drake. I intend to remedy that, to rebuild this organisation in a new form – a form more suited to the modern world and less susceptible to deception and corruption from within. If G.L.O.V.E. is to survive it must change and it must change quickly.'

'Do you really think we are going to just walk away?' another member of the council said. 'We are all here because we are powerful people. The resources and operations we control are what makes G.L.O.V.E. what it is, and if you do this we will fight you every inch of the way.'

'You are welcome to try,' Nero said, looking around the table. 'Many have. You may want to consider the fate that befell them before you seriously think about threatening me. I'm sure that I do not need to remind you that your identities are now known to the Americans, but what should concern you far more is that they are also known to the Disciples. Overlord may be dead but the organisation that supported him is still very much alive. If I were you, I would be less worried about waging war against me and more worried about finding an exceptionally good place to hide.'

'This is a coup, Nero,' Diaz said angrily.

'No,' Nero replied with ice in his voice, 'this is a cull. Quite literally for any of you that are foolish enough to oppose me.'

He stood up and looked around the table.

'This meeting is over. You will be transported back to your homes. I have no doubt that some of you will be thinking of fighting this or of coming after me. I will be waiting for you when you do.'

☹ ☹ ☹

Diabolus Darkdoom walked through the bustling corridors of H.I.V.E. Students in different coloured jumpsuits hurried to their lessons, a buzz of chatter and laughter filling the air. Nero had defeated many foes, steered many devious plans to completion, but H.I.V.E. was still his greatest achievement, Diabolus thought to himself. He walked down the corridor leading to Nero's office and pressed the button next to the door.

'Enter!' a voice called from inside.

'I've just come to say goodbye, Max,' Darkdoom said as he walked into the room. 'The Megalodon is ready for launch and I have things that I need to take care of.'

'You're sure I can't persuade you to stay?' Nero said, gesturing for his friend to take the seat on the other side of his desk. 'I'm always looking for new teachers and the students would benefit enormously from your experience.'

'Thank you, but no,' Darkdoom said with a grin. 'I'm not sure that I'm quite cut out for the academic life.'

'Well, if you should ever reconsider . . .' Nero said.

'I'll bear it in mind,' Darkdoom replied. 'Doctor Scott tells me that you're ignoring his medical advice as usual. How are you feeling?'

'Old,' Nero said with a wry smile, 'but I'm not quite ready for retirement yet. There's still too much to do.'

'How did the meeting with the ruling council go?' Darkdoom asked.

'About as well as you would expect,' Nero said with a sigh. 'Some of them are going to be trouble.'

'They were never all going to take it lying down,' Darkdoom replied with a small shrug. 'You're doing the right thing.'

'I hope you're right,' Nero said. 'I want to renew G.L.O.V.E., not destroy it.'

'The rose that is not pruned will not flower,' Darkdoom replied.

'A little poetic for my tastes, but I take your point,' Nero said with a wry smile. 'Diaz called it a coup. To be honest, there's a part of me that still wonders if she might be right.'

'Max, of all the senior members of G.L.O.V.E. that I have ever known, you are the only one who didn't actually want the job at the head of the table. The fact that you never wished to lead the council means that you're

278

the only one of us that can be trusted to do this. We need a fresh start, new blood.'

'It will not be easy,' Nero said.

'But you'll do it any way,' Darkdoom replied, standing up.

'Thank you again for your help, my friend,' Nero said, shaking Darkdoom's hand. 'Do you have any plans for what you're going to do next?'

'Yes, I'm going to see if I can find out more about our friends the Disciples,' Darkdoom replied. 'I fear that they will want revenge for what happened to Overlord.'

'Let me know what you discover,' Nero said, 'and be careful.'

'You know where I am if you need me,' Darkdoom said.

Darkdoom walked out of Nero's office and the door closed behind him. Nero sat back in his chair and stared at the stone carving of the G.L.O.V.E. symbol on the opposite wall. He knew that he had taken a huge risk by disbanding the ruling council but Darkdoom was right – it was a risk he had to take. The first task would be to decide who were the most suitable candidates to replace the ruling council. He needed capable people who he knew he could trust – a rare commodity in the world he inhabited. He reached into his desk drawer and took out a piece of paper. Listed on it were the names of all of the former

Alphas who had survived the mission to destroy Overlord. He picked up the pen from his desk and, after staring at the list for a minute or two, he slowly began to underline names.

☢ ☢ ☢

Duncan Cavendish sat at his desk, reading the notes that had been prepared for him ahead of Prime Minister's Questions in the House of Commons. His phone rang and he answered it after a few seconds.

'Yes,' he said impatiently.

'I have a call on your private line, Prime Minister,' his secretary said. 'He wouldn't give his name, he just said he was an old friend.'

'Put it through,' Cavendish said, frowning. 'Hello?'

'Hello, Prime Minister. It's so good to speak to you again,' the voice on the other end said.

'Nero,' Cavendish whispered.

'You sound surprised to hear from me,' Nero said, 'I wonder why?'

'I suppose you've called to threaten me,' Cavendish said. 'Don't waste your breath. My security detail is second to none. You can't touch me.'

'Oh, I'm not going to hurt you physically,' Nero said. 'I'm going to make you do something far more painful. I'm going to make you resign.'

'And why on earth would I do that?' Cavendish asked.

'Because if you don't, I'm going to send several eminent journalists all the information that they'll need to reveal the cover-up regarding your . . . *education*.'

'You can't do that,' Cavendish replied, an edge of panic in his voice.

'I'm sure that the British public will be intrigued to discover that their Prime Minister cannot account for six years of his life,' Nero said. 'I can almost see the headlines now.'

'I'll expose you,' Cavendish spat. 'I'll tell the world about H.I.V.E. if you do this.'

'Oh really,' Nero replied. 'So presumably you'll tell them that actually you didn't go to a top private school and you did, in fact, attend a secret school of global villainy that's housed inside a volcano but you've got no idea where it actually is. That should go down well.'

Cavendish felt his heart sink. He had been a politician for long enough to know when his opponent was holding all the cards.

'You have twenty-four hours,' Nero said. 'I'd go with wanting to spend more time with your family, if I were you. I believe that's traditional.'

The line went dead. Cavendish looked around his office, surveying all that he had worked so hard to attain.

He pulled a sheet of headed paper from his desk drawer, picked up his pen and began to write.

☹ ☹ ☹

Otto sat alone on the sofa in the accommodation block, staring off into space. Hard as he tried he could not stop mentally replaying the events of their final confrontation with Overlord. He knew it would do no good to dwell on the what ifs and maybes of what happened, but that did not change the fact that he desperately wished that things could have turned out differently. Laura sat down on the seat next to him, looking at him with a slightly worried expression.

'I'd ask what you were thinking about but I'm fairly sure I already know,' Laura said softly. 'It wasn't your fault.'

'Wasn't it?' Otto said with a sigh.

'No, it wasn't,' Laura said. 'You didn't pull the trigger, you didn't choose to be there. It was Overlord – it was always him.'

'Maybe,' Otto said, looking at Laura, 'but if it hadn't been for me, Lucy wouldn't have been there – none of you would have been there. Who's it going to be next time? You? Wing? Shelby?'

'Otto,' Laura said, putting her hand on his, 'this isn't you. You know what I – what we all love about you? You're the strongest of all of us. You're the glue that holds us all together and none of us want to see you like this.

Overlord's gone, for good this time, and you have *your* life back. Now you just have to start living it again.'

'I suppose you're right,' Otto said, 'but I can't shake this feeling that Lucy traded her future for mine.'

'Maybe she did,' Laura said, 'and if that's true the worst, most selfish thing you could do is waste what she has given you. Everything you get to do from this point onwards is thanks to her. Don't think about what might have been, think about what's going to be. That's all she would have wanted.'

Otto stared at Laura for a moment and then nodded.

'You're right,' he said. 'Thanks.'

'I'm always right – I learnt that from you,' Laura said with a wink, glancing over his shoulder. 'Look out – here come the lovebirds.'

Wing and Shelby were walking across the atrium together. They had been inseparable since returning to H.I.V.E., despite the fact that they were quite possibly the least obviously compatible couple in human history.

'Hey, guys,' Shelby said as she sat down opposite Laura and Otto. 'Wanna hear something funny?'

'It is not funny,' Wing said as he sat down next to her, looking slightly embarrassed.

'Are you kidding? It's hilarious,' Shelby said with a grin. 'Guess who got taken down by Franz in the combat simulation this morning?'

'You're joking,' Otto said in disbelief, as Wing just closed his eyes and shook his head.

'There I was, backing him up, and our friend here's doing his usual sneaky stealth thing when suddenly, out of nowhere, BOOM! Head shot. No more Mr Ninja guy,' Shelby explained with delight.

'He eliminated you too,' Wing said, avoiding eye contact with Laura and Otto.

'Yeah, well, it's hard to hit anything when you're laughing so much that you can't breathe,' Shelby said, grinning from ear to ear.

'And so the ritual humiliation begins,' Wing said with a sigh, rolling his eyes.

'You know you love it,' Shelby said, leaning over and giving him a peck on the cheek.

'Franz ought to be more careful,' Laura said. 'If not he'll end up on H.I.V.E.mind's list and the next thing he knows he'll be standing in a hangar somewhere with no clue why he's there.'

'Thanks for reminding me,' Otto said. 'I've got enough circuitry in my head without Nero implanting a computerised dog whistle in my skull on graduation day.'

'I shouldn't worry, Otto,' Shelby said with a grin. 'H.I.V.E.mind only activated the Alphas who'd be any use in a fight. You're perfectly safe. On the other hand, if he ever needs his hard drive defragmented – well, then you're really in trouble.'

'I'd laugh,' Otto said, smiling back at Shelby, 'but recently I've been trying to do that only when someone says something that's actually funny.'

'Personally, I found the Zero Hour plan rather disturbing,' Wing said with a slight frown.

'Aye, it is a wee bit creepy,' Laura said.

'At least we'll never know if Nero's actually done it to us,' Otto replied.

'And that's less creepy because . . .' Shelby said.

'OK, more creepy, way more creepy,' Otto admitted. 'Probably best not to think about it at all.'

Nigel walked up to them with a slightly worried expression on his face.

'Erm . . . guys, Franz is just over at the snack machine,' he said nervously. 'I thought I should warn you that his win in the combat simulation has – well, gone to his head slightly.'

'What do you mean?' Laura asked.

'You'll see,' Nigel replied.

Franz was walking across the atrium tucking into a packet of crisps. There was a definite swagger in his step.

'Hey, Franz,' Shelby said as he approached.

'Franz? There is no Franz,' he said with a dismissive

shake of his head. 'From now on you shall be using the new nickname that I am choosing –' He pointed his fingers at Wing in the shape of a gun – 'Silent Death.'

They did stop laughing . . . eventually.

☻ ☻ ☻

Which Stream are you?

- ALPHA
- HENCHMAN
- TECHNICAL
- POLITICAL / FINANCIAL

Turn over to begin the test . . .

Answer the following questions to find out which stream you belong in.

I. If you were an animal, which of the following would you be?

A. Panther
B. Rhino
C. Spider
D. Snake

2. How might you make one of your enemies sorry?

A. With a hypnotic trigger phrase – so that every time someone says 'Pass the salt', they cluck like a chicken
B. Break every bone in their body – even the ones they didn't know existed
C. Rewire their alarm clock so that it always goes off at 4 a.m.
D. Discover their most embarrassing secret, and publicly expose it – after blackmailing them for a brief, yet lucrative, period

3. If you could choose any instrument to aid you in your villainous cause, what would it be?

A. Nothing – your cunning is all you will ever need
B. A bazooka
C. A computer
D. Money – after all, it is the root of all evil

4. You decide to take over your school. How would you achieve this?

A. Simply inform the headmaster that you are indisputably the most qualified person for the job – you had read every book in the library by the time you were four years old, and have a better understanding of the subjects than the teachers do

B. Threaten to show the headmaster what his/her spleen looks like if control of the school is not relinquished immediately

C. Hack into the computer system and rewrite all of the school's files to show that you are, in fact, already the headmaster

D. Infiltrate the local council and appoint yourself as Head of Education – why settle for just your school?

If your answers are mostly As . . .
Alpha: The Alpha stream specialises in leadership and strategy training. You exhibit certain unique abilities which mark you out as one of the leaders of tomorrow.

If your answers are mostly Bs
Henchman: Your aggression knows no bounds, and you are happiest when you're doing damage to something, or more likely, someone. Your uncluttered, uncomplicated mind makes you the perfect trusted subordinate.

If your answers are mostly Cs
Technical: There's not a computer that you cannot hack, or a bomb you cannot defuse (or build, for that matter). You put the 'EEK!' in computer geek.

If your answers are mostly Ds
Political/Financial: You have a brilliant head for figures (as well as ways to fudge them), and also happen to be excessively charming and a natural born liar – the perfect combination for a successfully sinister career in politics or finance.

Your Stream has been selected. Now take the test to discover how villainous you are...

1. You find a wallet on the floor filled with ten pound notes, do you:

A. Immediately take the wallet to the police and hand it over, still filled with the money

B. Help yourself to some of the money and then take it to the police

C. Take the money, throw the wallet in the bin and spend the cash on stolen blueprints for the nearest bank

2. You see a small child eating your favourite ice cream, do you:

A. Ask the child where he got the ice cream and set off to buy your own

B. Explain to the child that ice cream is bad for the teeth and make them feel guilty enough to hand it over

C. Organise two henchmen to suspend the small child upside down over a duck pond while you enjoy the icy goodness of their treat

3. Your parents agree to buy you any birthday present you want, do you ask for:

A. Nothing, you would rather your parents treated themselves

B. A new hi-fi and games system so you can lock yourself away in your bedroom

C. A small island in the middle of the Pacific, fully equipped with secret hideout, submarine base and lasers

4. When buying a new house what room is your priority?

A. An ecologically sound conservatory

B. A huge communications room so you can spy on your nearest and dearest

C. An underground lair complete with torture devices and a shark-filled pool

5. You have a red button in front of you that you have been told never to press, do you:

A. Quietly read a book, never giving the button a second thought

B. Stroke the button gently, always feeling tempted to give it a good push

C. Instantly press the button – you built this doomsday device so why shouldn't you use it!

6. An army of robots is about to take over your town, do you:

A. Find a way to foil the robots and destroy them for ever

B. Find a way to foil the robots but keep one just in case you might need it one day

C. Find a way to foil the robots because frankly your army of GIANT SPACE ROBOTS will do a better job

7. You need to hire a henchman, who do you hire:

A. Your mum

B. A couple of ex-cons you found through eBay

C. A suitably subservient weakling who will bow to your every needs . . . and a GIANT SPACE ROBOT

8. You have captured your heroic foe and can at last be rid of him, do you:

A. Have a change of heart, let him go and give yourself up to the authorities
B. Give the hero five minutes to escape from a shrinking room while making a quick getaway
C. Take a long time to explain your convoluted plans for ruling the world, realise the hero has escaped and send your GIANT SPACE ROBOT after him

If your answers are mostly As . . .

To be fair you don't really have a villainous bone in your body. In fact, I suspect you would rather share a cup of tea with your foe, talk about old times and generally have a nice time. It's probably best to give up villainy now and try something more suited to your needs, say knitting or looking after bunnies.

If your answers are mostly Bs . . .

OK, so you have some villainous traits but you're not quite ready for big time yet. You're the kind of villainous soul that would pull only half the legs off a spider so they would have some chance of getting away. With a little training you could be a decent villain but you're no way ready for the big league.

If your answers are mostly Cs . . .

Hello future megalomaniac and ruler of the world. You are a vile villain through and through. You've probably got some plans to take over the world hidden in a draw somewhere and if you haven't already undergone training in Applied Villainy at H.I.V.E. then you should be applying for a place now. Oh, and I hear that GIANT SPACE ROBOTS are currently half-price at your local superstore.

Details of H.I.V.E. students and instructors for your Villainous files

STUDENTS

Otto Malpense
Orphaned at birth, Otto is a criminal genius with a limitless mind, photographic memory and rare extra-sensory skills. Using a robotic mind control device he coerced the British Prime Minister into mooning at a press conference, and ended up in H.I.V.E.

Wing Fanchu
Otto's best friend, Wing was recruited into H.I.V.E. due to his exceptional skill in martial arts and numerous forms of selfdefence.

Laura Brand
Laura has an uncanny expertise with computers, so much so that she made it into H.I.V.E. by hacking into an US military airbase in order to use their military frequency to find out if one of her friends was gossiping about her behind her back.

Shelby Trinity
This all American girl is actually a world renowned jewel thief known as The Wraith. Shelby stole her way into H.I.V.E.

Nigel Darkdoom
It's tough following in your father's footsteps, particularly when you're small and bald and your dad is the infamous criminal mastermind Diabolus Darkdoom. Nigel has a lot to live up to. He does, however, have a talent for science and a strange affinity with plants.

Franz Argentblum
Franz is son and heir to the largest manufacturer of chocolate in Europe. Like Nigel, his father is also a criminal mastermind. Franz is most easily recognised by his impressive size and strong German accent.

Lucy Dexter
The granddaughter of the Contessa (deceased) and has inherited her special talent for mind control.

INSTRUCTORS

Dr Nero
Dr Maximilian Nero is the founder and headmaster of H.I.V.E. He also happens to be one of the most ruthless and devious men alive, and is a senior member of G.L.O.V.E.

Raven
Natalya (a.k.a. Raven) is the most feared assassin in H.I.V.E. She was originally trained in infiltration and counter-intelligence in Russia. She has a long, curved scar that runs down one cheek, although very few people would know as most people she 'encounters' rarely get a chance to make note of their assailant's appearance before they lose consciousness (if they are lucky).

Colonel Francisco
Head of the Tactical Educational department, Colonel Francisco is thought by the students to be one of the toughest teachers at H.I.V.E.

Professor Pike
Head of the Science and Technology department, Professor Pike may appear disorganised and distracted, but appearances are often deceiving. He is one of the original creators of H.I.V.E.mind.

Ms Leon
Currently, her consciousness is trapped in the body of her fluffy white cat (with special thanks to Professor Pike). Tabitha Leon is an expert at infiltration and counter-surveillance. She teaches Stealth and Evasion at H.I.V.E.

H.I.V.E.mind
H.I.V.E.mind is a first generation artificially intelligent entity and the school's omnipresent super-computer. The purpose of H.I.V.E.mind is to serve and ensure the uninterrupted functioning of the school.

Join the world's most talented villains for more incredible adventures at H.I.V.E. It would be criminal not to . . .

Thirteen-year-old master criminal Otto Malpense has been chosen to attend H.I.V.E., the top-secret school of Villainy. But there's one small catch – he cannot leave until his training is complete. He's left with one option. Escape. He just needs to figure out how.

A new power is rising to challenge Number One, the most formidable villain alive. But who is it? And why do they want to assassinate Otto Malpense, star pupil of H.I.V.E., and his best friend, Wing Fanchu?

H.I.V.E. is in grave danger. Dr Nero, its leader, has been captured by the world's most ruthless security force. It's up to Otto to save him, but first he must escape from Nero's sinister replacement.

One of the world's most powerful villains is threatening global Armageddon, and Otto, Wing and his most trusted villain-friends find themselves in the sights of the most dangerous man alive, with nowhere to run to.

Otto Malpense, star pupil at the top-secret school for Villainy, has gone rogue. In a deadly race against time, Raven and Wing must find Otto before the order to eliminate him can be carried out.

The evil A.I. Overlord is about to put his terrible plans into action. Then no one will be able to stand in his way. It is time to activate Zero Hour, a plan designed to eliminate any villain on the brink of global domination.

Are you ready for Otto's new mind-blowing adventure?

'Artemis Fowl would fit in perfectly at H.I.V.E.' EOIN COLFER

MARK WALDEN

H·I·V·E

Aftershock

BLOOMSBURY

Otto and the rest of the elite Alpha stream have been sent on their most dangerous exercise yet: The Hunt. But when Otto and the Alphas arrive in the icy wastes of Siberia, it becomes clear that something is wrong. There's a traitor in their midst, and time is running out to discover who it is.